GW00674714

## THE HIGH PRIESTESS
## NEVER MARRIES

Sharanya Manivannan's first book of poetry, *Witchcraft*, was described in *The Straits Times* as 'sensuous and spiritual, delicate and dangerous and as full as the moon reflected in a knife'. She was specially commissioned to write and perform a poem at the 2015 Commonwealth Day Observance in London.

*The High Priestess Never Marries* is her first work of fiction.

Sharanya
Manivannan

# THE
# HIGH
# PRIESTESS
# NEVER
# MARRIES

*Stories of*
*Love and Consequence*

HarperCollins *Publishers* India

First published in hardback in India in 2016 by
HarperCollins *Publishers* India

Copyright © Sharanya Manivannan 2016

P-ISBN: 978-93-5264-088-1
E-ISBN: 978-93-5264-089-8

2 4 6 8 10 9 7 5 3 1

Sharanya Manivannan asserts the moral right
to be identified as the author of this work.

**HarperCollins *Publishers***
A-75, Sector 57, Noida, Uttar Pradesh 201301, India
1 London Bridge Street, London, SE1 9GF, United Kingdom
Hazelton Lanes, 55 Avenue Road, Suite 2900, Toronto, Ontario M5R 3L2
*and* 1995 Markham Road, Scarborough, Ontario M1B 5M8, Canada
25 Ryde Road, Pymble, Sydney, NSW 2073, Australia
195 Broadway, New York, NY 10007, USA

Typeset in 10/14 Sabon by
R. Ajith Kumar

Printed and bound at
Thomson Press (India) Ltd.

# CONTENTS

*'a vixen's courage in vixen terms'*
*Adrienne Rich*

*sviya (Sanskrit): she who is her own wife*

'I don't know why he's angry with me.'

'I don't know why anyone would be angry with you.'

'That's sweet of you. It's true though – these men…'

'You know how they say Rama was so brilliant that every monkey in his army wanted to marry him?'

'And so he said to them, "I'll see you in my next life…"'

'And thus they became Krishna's sixteen thousand gopikas.'

'I haven't got another life to spare. I have Ketu in the twelfth house. This is my last dance.'

'A pity.'

'Oh, but I have lives yet to live in this one.'

'So perhaps all these people, at some point or the other, really just wanted to be—'

'My wife.'

'And so, tigerlily, you have to fulfil whatever it was you promised them, which was probably eternal love.'

'Everyone I have ever loved I have loved eternally. Each love a life in itself.'

'That's a lot of dying.'

'That's a lot of resurrection.'

# SELF-PORTRAIT WITHOUT MYTHOLOGY

That's the thing about this business. Some days you sparkle like a teenage vampire. Some days you feel as though you've walked through the remains of an exploded dhrishti pusanika, which is to say, fucked. Most days, however, you pick out one item from your collection of lungis appropriated from men you have slept with, pin your hair up, cook your own lunch, and try not to think about it.

Now and then you buy yourself a single red African daisy from a flower seller on the street. Sometimes you put it behind your ear. Sometimes you just keep it someplace where you can look at it.

You count on very little to run like clockwork, except perhaps the power cuts. Time exists only if you stop to ponder it, and it's rarely wise to do this. It seems you were always here, long before

1

you even arrived. Orbiting. Pivoting on a constant.
You can go for months without entering the sea,
but there is no given moment when you cannot
point out its precise cardinal direction. All of it
is deep within your being, if not your body itself
– sweetness, slow dancing, the knowledge that
grief has no after, places of pilgrimage, exigencies,
seasons of plenitude, red-light districts, the
memory of mountains.

Some things are important to you. These you
must count frequently. There must be music. There
must be something to drink. You love the sound of
the human voice, and as difficult as you are, there
are a few people for whom there will always be
places at your table.

You number among what you own: a
gramophone, a small, seated bronze Parvati –
solitary, her left foot extended, her inguina open
– and your grandmother's thaali. You number
among that which you share your life with, but
do not possess: windowsill cacti, visiting omens,
other people's children, full and eclipsed moons,
books, the company of trees, owls.

There are no good photographs of you laughing
from when your teeth were still crooked, but in
your old age you hope to be wild-eyed, white-
haired, a fearsome and fabulous crone. You think

of old age often. On the most recondite of days the future shows itself to you in the blink of an eye. You are already there. You have always been here.

You are superstitious about the handling of knives, farewells and palli dosham.

You have few rules for this particular life that has become yours, but each is of consequence. Be observant but not vigilant, for the time for terror has passed. Love anyway. Praise every landscape that appears before your window; hold in equal measure the beauty of a cyclone and the miracle of a single woodpecker on a swaying coconut tree. Bear witness. Nothing lasts forever, and nothing is lost. Avoid regret. Love, any way.

## GREED AND THE GANDHI QUARTET

The moment you name a craving is the moment it annexes everything. It happens as we leave the temple, pausing somewhere halfway down its three hundred and sixty-five steps to catch our breaths and enjoy the view. I see the monkey on the banister and my stomach stirs with something more complex than hunger. I stop talking. Tail a question mark in mid-air, it scrapes its teeth on a seed almost pared of fruit, its eyes absorbed, not without pleasure.

'It's just eating a mango stone, di,' he says. 'Just a stone.'

But it is not a stone, it is a seed. I look at my friend, pious as a penitent and sincere as a second wife. The ash on his forehead puckers in disbelief. I realize my eyes are wet.

'It's not that, it's just the gesture, the cupping

of the hands and the lowering of the head. It just reminds me of…'

He coughs exaggeratedly. 'Ahem. Lady, this is a holy place.'

'It's just the filling, the feasting, that sort of deep hunger.'

He has taken me by the elbow and steered me away; we are once again descending the steps sloping the hillock to the village below us, where his driver snoozes with the car doors open. Overhead, the clouds do little to undercut the late morning heat. 'Okay, just what does it remind you of?'

'Gorging on grief.'

'Ugh, why?'

We have come to Thiruthani so that he can make a vow. It has many tiers: if he finds a boyfriend within a year, he will come back with an offering of fruit, flowers and five hundred rupees. If he moves in with him, he will endow an abhishegam. If his boyfriend has a convenient passport which allows matrimony, he will carry a kavadi and distribute alms to one hundred and eight needy people.

'Needy people?' I'd scoffed then. 'Try all the exes of all my exes.'

'Because grief is sweet,' I say now. 'It serrates the edges of the senses. You feel everything in technicolour. The universe begins to speak to you like some...'

'Pentecostal?'

I laugh. It's an allusion to the upbringing he ran away from.

I come to a stop, look him in the eye and squeeze his hand. 'I should have made a vow too.'

He rolls his eyes. 'Impeccable timing as usual! Couldn't you have thought of this half an hour ago?'

'No, really.' I take a deep breath. 'What if I wake up in twenty years regretting what I didn't do now?'

'Like what?'

'Like settle down, put down roots.'

'All this while, you've been saying that what you want is love and partnership. Not being tied down. Not buying gold jewellery. Not legally binding contracts. None of the things us mortals want, know we want and say we want.'

'Well, what if I'm wrong?'

He sighs. 'Listen, you're just overwhelmed. Think about it for a year or two. What's that to you anyway? That's usually how long you take to pine over a single failed affair.'

'Ouch – thanks!'

'Sweetheart,' he says. 'Don't take this the wrong way, but you are crazy.'

'So are you!'

'Wrong,' he says with impregnable assurance. 'You're crazy. You want things you don't even want. I, on the other hand, have always wanted what I've always wanted. You're crazy, but I'm the one who'll get committed.'

~

A year passes this way. No boyfriends materialize for either of us.

One day we bump into someone who insists we accompany him to a crafts exhibition at Valluvarkottam, the piss-drenched monolith in the middle of the city. When we lose him on the sidewalk, we realize the invitation was not truly meant to be taken seriously, but we carry on anyway. I keep my eyes open for the woman I have seen on dozens of previous occasions, always catching sight of her from inside a vehicle headed elsewhere, without ever having been impulsive enough to stop.

And yet, today, here I am and here she isn't, the turmeric-faced teller of fortunes I have wanted for so long to speak to.

'I want to ask her about my love life.'

'Nothing else?'

'No, just that. Work and all that, I know I'll manage somehow. But love…'

'… is not in our hands.'

We enter the exhibit – I buy for him a set of terracotta teacups and a pot with two spouts resembling the horns of a cow. 'Double-pronged, just the way I like it.' He winks at the merchant to seal the joke and accepts his confusion graciously.

For me he buys bangles: dragonfruit-pink and myna-beak yellow. I put them on immediately. 'If I get skinny with sorrow, they will fall from my wrists and into the river while I bathe, like in the old poems,' I sigh.

He snorts. 'No chance, O Nitambavati of the Cooum. I have beheld you as you devoured breakfast.'

He is fasting. In supplication. Now there's only one tier: boyfriend, boyfriend, boyfriend.

'When I was in love with the American…'

'You mean your Jewish lover from Noo Yawk City?'

'Stop talking to my Auroville friends. They never forget anything.'

'Which is why you still live here, at the end of the day. That and yours truly.'

'And you'll abscond the first chance *you* get.'

'True, that. So go on. The American…'

'He had a thing for monkeys. So … you know Gandhi's monkeys – see no evil, speak no evil, hear no evil? I found him a wooden set, a paperweight that had a fourth.' I pause for effect but not so long as to give him the punchline. 'The fourth monkey had its hands over its crotch.'

He laughs.

'Good advice, no?'

'Indeed. Put that on the birthday wishlist.'

'You mean the wedding registry.'

'Really, a paperweight? For my wedding? Cheapness.'

'And pray tell: what are you buying me for my wedding?'

'A husband, most likely. I think you'll find one a most delightful accompaniment to your conjugal life.'

I laugh just a second too late. He frowns. 'What happened?'

'Nothing, I just remembered…'

'What, di?'

'Do you remember that monkey we saw when we went to Thiruthani?'

'What monkey?'

'The one gnawing on a mango seed. The one I was transfixed by.'

'Okay … What about it?'

'Well, listen. What it had actually reminded me of was the way Bear used to eat. Like he'd been hungry for years. At every meal. It was adorable, actually. I mean I' – shit, my voice is breaking – 'I cooked for him all the time.'

He nods, slowly understanding.

'I made a mistake.'

'He treated you badly. I know that. That's all that counts to me.'

'But … if he comes back…'

'No.'

'What?'

'No. I forbid it. You're not doing that again.'

'Well,' I say ruefully. 'It's not like he will come back.'

He doesn't answer right away, and when he does, he sounds exasperated. 'You always want the things you don't want. Why is that?'

'Maybe it's because I can't have the things I do want.'

'Don't cry here. Come on. Let's go.'

He leads me out of the hall of shops and back on to the main road. My fortune teller is still nowhere in sight, but there is an old woman selling forearm-lengths of pungent orange jasmine. She calls out to us and holds out a thick strand. 'No, thanks,' he says. 'Not today.'

'Today only,' she says. 'Take it. It's for you. No charge.'

I hesitate.

'Poor thing. What did you do, scold her? Worse? Women are meant to be coddled, don't you know?'

'I know,' he says. 'Believe me, I know.' He accepts the flowers and thanks her, then coils them into my topknot right away, garnering an appreciative chortle, betel-stained and blessing-filled.

'Now you'll have to invite her to your wedding,' he says into my ear.

'She can come to all of my weddings,' I gush. 'All of them.'

~

From my kitchen window on the third floor, we spy a green parrot perched between two crows on an unmoving rib of coconut leaves. This is what I know, after years of studying them: the omens are not meant to be read as portents of his return. They are meant only to help me live with what is present: choices and consequences, chaos and deceptive calm, his absence.

I make tea, black and sugary with cardamom, and pass two freshly washed cups to my friend. We have decided to inaugurate the terracotta set. We clink, make a toast.

'To afternoon tea.'

'To royalty.'

'To afternoon sex.'

'To loyalty.'

We sip, both smiling, aware we have just concocted an anthem for future tea ceremonies.

'You know,' he starts. 'I don't really know if that's the right way to live, like those monkeys. The Gandhi Quartet. Not seeing, not listening, not saying, not doing.'

'Yeah, I guess not. Even if "fuck no evil" is probably a good code to live by.'

'You're the one who's always talking about living with intensity, feeling everything. How can you do that if you're blindfolded or gagged or chastity-belted or whatever it is?'

'You're right, you can't.'

'But even you did it for a while.'

I look out of the window, and there is a white-footed black cat on the ledge of the adjacent rooftop. I see it every day. It never leaps.

'Everything reminds you of Bear. Even though I know you loved the American more.'

'Maybe that's true.'

'And I know others have made you happier.' He skims over this sentence like a skater on ice or a bird over water, as though the dark depths beneath it hold no pull.

'Maybe it's just that no one else ever made me so wretchedly sad.'

'You always want what you don't want, don't you? Not even what you can't have or shouldn't want, but simply do not want. Every single time.'

~

We go to the beach at a too-early hour, the sky still sun-bleached, blotted only by crows. Another six months have passed. The temple visits have dwindled. He is involved with a married man. He says it's just for now.

He has taken off his rudraksha rosary. I have begun to wear nuptial toe-rings. In public, I might be safer because of them. To be married is to be above reproach.

We buy paper cones of boiled chickpeas with onions. Then roasted corn, scorched in places with a blackness more savoury than you might think.

Then, as more vendors open their shops, cotton candy. We cannot stop eating. We roll up our pants to the knees and take turns stepping into the water while the other watches the sandals and bags. Women with divining sticks pass us, offer us our own futures. We decline like optimists, or nihilists.

We carry bottles of juice spiked with rum. 'Babe,' I begin, somewhere around sunset. 'But don't you ever think about how much you wanted something else, and what you've settled for? I mean, for me, it wasn't so much a case of missing the bus but rather a case of not buying a ticket at all. You … always wanted more.'

He doesn't take his eyes off the tides.

'But you don't have to listen to me since I am a padupaavi,' I say.

'Good god, this again. Woman. We've been going over this for like a year. Why are you still guilty? You didn't cheat on him. He treated you like shit and you knew deep down he was going to leave you and so you went, like anyone would, to someone who actually made you feel wanted.'

'I was greedy, that's what I was. I had him at that point. Why did I need further validation?'

'Additionally, you keep forgetting that he constantly claimed to be some kind of postmodern libertine who didn't believe in institutions or the concept of infidelity because he didn't believe, to begin with, in the concept of fidelity. So how exactly, tell me once again for good measure, was it cheating?'

'It was cheating because I loved him, that's all.'

He looks at me first with pity and then with something more nuanced. 'You really are a pathini, all said and done, aren't you?' He kisses my cheek and hugs me sideways.

'Careful, we're going to get arrested.'

'What fun – an adventure! That's what life's all about, right?'

'Right.' I smile.

'Of course I want more. You think it doesn't tear me to pieces to think of him with his wife every night, while I wrap my arms around a bolster?'

'The morning after the first time I ever slept over, Bear told me that he missed his ex's body in the bed beside him. I don't know if I ever told you that.'

Something unbearable crosses his face. He looks away for a moment, then says thoughtfully, 'But this is the love that is before me right now. Who am I to say no?'

'What about autonomy? Volition?'

'What about vulnerability, receptivity?'

'God, it's just so hard.'

'It is. How do you strike a balance? How do

you know when it's God talking, or your gut...'

'... or just greed?'

We watch the waves for a few minutes. I trace figure eights, infinity analemmas, in the sand with my big toe. 'Hey, you know what?' I suddenly recall. 'This guy once tried to break up with me here.'

'What, on the beach?'

'At the Gandhi statue!'

'Haha, really?'

'Yes. I mean, he asked me to meet him at the Gandhi statue and then take a stroll down "to enjoy the sea breeze". And I knew he was going to dump me, so I said to him, "And do you really think that I won't slap you just because we're standing under the Gandhi statue?"'

He laughs. 'And?'

'Well, no further discussion, really. That was it. Can you imagine, if I'd come here with him, I'd have been so traumatized I'd have avoided the Marina for years.'

'God, yeah ... Knowing you...'

'I know, right? Jerk.'

He grunts. 'Sometimes I wonder what the point of all these cool life stories is if I'll never have grandkids to tell them to.'

'Yeah, so do I.'

'But you know, di, I do think you're right – volition and all that. We have to take some responsibility, right? It's just so fucking jarring, though, when the smallest thing, something so utterly negligible, winds up rattling you to your core. And you wish you hadn't said yes to one blind date, one unprotected fuck, one more drink.'

I get up, dust the sand off my bum, and give him my hand.

'We did this to ourselves, it's true.'

He doesn't say anything. We walk for a few minutes along the shore in silence, linking fingers lightly.

And at a moment of perfect chiaroscuro, we step once again into the water to watch the sun sink into it, languorous as molasses. His mood lightens. 'Oh, isn't it lovely sometimes to feel like a mermaid basking on the beach, all your world lapping at your flipper feet?'

And he drops his cigarette on the sand and the sea goes up in flames.

# SCHEHERAZADE ON THE SHORE

There must be other places like it, secret ones, even in this city that allows no one to keep their own. That night, we took the elevator to the rooftop bar – six floors high – in a hotel so shady that almost no one remembers its existence, even though it hunkered neon on the main road, one swoop of a crow's coast to the beach. We were the first ones there, at twilight, and as the evening deepened, the crowd around us thickened and shifted. We took the farthest table on the balcony and ordered rum and Coke, and sides of chicken skewered with pineapple and cheese.

You, of course, had never been there before. Only two categories of people who knew the bar existed: those whom I took there, and those whose orbits and mine never intersected – men whose faces could never be seen in those shadows.

Desire shimmered between us, like light

inflected on a surface too opaque to plunge into. But you – you had never been. Plunged into, I mean. The burden of restraint was mine. Apologies are always a thousand, or none. I wanted to tell you something about myself, and so I told you a fable about red giraffes.

'The red giraffes were eagerly awaited. The crowds arrived a whole hour early, and lined both sides of the long cordoned road with their anticipation and impatience. Little children sat on their fathers' shoulders and made petulant demands. Short women staked out the higher levels of the footpath and idled there in their dark glasses, sipping juice, scanning the scene like sentinels. Young men straddled the road divider and tipped their weights over to one side, placing their feet in nooks in the metal that would allow them to stand, elevated, when they wanted to. The city had cleared its roads and shaken off its torpor for this. Even the subtle mid-January sunset took an especially slow curtsy that evening, as if it knew that none of the waiting that enlivened the breeze was for anything as ordinary as nightfall. But the giraffes, in spite of being of a distant imagination, had thought it wise to acclimatize, and so themselves arrived almost an hour late.

'At the far end of the road, a drum roll

reverberated. Long elegant limbs straightened themselves. Red necks uncurled like stamens. A woman inside a tarpaulin belly finished breast-feeding and passed her baby to a waiting friend with a kiss. A man crawled into the space beside her and gave her the thumbs-up sign. An opera singer as pretty as a doll opened her voice like she was unrolling a carpet. The red giraffes were ready.

'But no sooner had they taken a few stilted steps down the avenue that had been cleared and policed for their parade than the first of them got their necks tangled in the electric wires. It happened over and over.

'Strangulated, the red giraffes kicked their mechanical legs like they were in real pain. Their bodies kept trying to move but their heads were trapped. Though not a sound came out of their elongated throats, if you looked at them, they seemed to be screaming.

'Each time this happened, after what seemed like a protracted agony, men with ladders and elaborate contrivances would extricate the giraffes from the wires, holding the wires apart as the giraffes manoeuvred their heads out of capture.

'When they disentangled themselves, all the pretty lights in the trees came down with them.

And they shook, bewildered, as though their costume hides held some feral, frightened core.

'And then they would take, uncertainly, a few more steps.

'Like all beautiful things in this city, the red giraffes too learnt to keep their heads down.

'The parade took a long time to end, and when it was over, not all the giraffes could remember how to raise themselves upright again. A few would always remember; and in their sleep, if nowhere else, their chins would rise and their shoulders would fall back and for a few blissful minutes, they were glorious again.

'The difficulty of leaving can sometimes be the same thing as the decision to stay. So let us say, then, that they decided to stay on in the city, quietly gathering an armoury of adjustments. They grew to like the taste of steam that rose from the tarmac throughout the year, and the brown monsoons that clogged the city's arteries for brief, flood-full weeks. They fell in line with the endless, easy cacophony of squat aspirations. They befriended trees at their root levels, and found them less appetizing but better conversationalists than the leaves they used to know (but oh, on certain days, how they missed the leaves they used to know!). After a while, the sun puckered the shine off their skins and their eyelids grew more hooded. Their spines sloped in attractive gradients, which they learnt to decorate with low-lying flora. When the red giraffes sat down, they crossed their legs, the awkward angles of their limbs jutting, like gauche remarks, into spaces not their own. Sometimes, they turned their still graceful necks to gaze out of windows and caught themselves wondering, struggling to remember what they had once known to call the sky.'

As if on cue, the lights went out in the bar. By the time they came back, one or both of us – which version do you prefer? – had disappeared.

When I told you this story I was looking at the moon in ascent, lifting its ripe immaculate weight out of the sea, but it was my face you looked at the whole time.

Perhaps I told you this story as a way of giving you this bar on the shore with its windows of net, through which I had lassoed that moon on so many nights. That transaction was irrevocable. But perhaps I told you this story so that I could be prudent with the ones I didn't tell, the ones that would take more. More nights. Less camouflage, fewer nets that sieved more than they seized. More than just selenic impulse or the way liquor glints with false numinosity under certain promises, certain lights. You were right: I had done this before. Not everyone was worth the trust. Not everyone survived the tellings.

# CONCHOLOGY

### Sarala Kali

Sarala Kali and I would sit in the water and talk. We would wander down serried in the early dusk and settle by the sea, draw a circle in the sand and step into it. We would let our feet be licked by its tongues in the pink of evening, and then as the height of the surges rose we would not move inland. The sea would swirl around us, our hands bangle-deep in the sand. Like this we would stay, cold and warm at once, until in the night's ink I could almost not see her any more. And then we would be all teeth and sclera and the glitter of zircon in our nostrils, earthbound by our ocean-drenched weights.

Some nights we would even lie supine, and somehow I could still hear her through the deluge of waves in my ears. My tears would fall off the sides of my face and into the sea I lay in. My hair would become a bushel of salt.

And her laughter, it would shake the moon.

## Tiruvallikeni

They say that this was once a forest of lotuses within a forest of holy basil. Now it is a slum, bisected by a river, with a train station with an ancient name. All that still exists of its holy geography is the sea beyond these lost forests. It still shatters itself here, where the women gather to sing to their dead. They beat their breasts to create rhythm. They crack their voices open like eggshells, inflaming revelation. This is the truth: it is not relief that the mourning songs provide. It is sheer revelation. All else but grief is stripped away. Grief is the only stage. Grief, the only witness.

I would go to the slum by the sea to listen to their songs. I would pay them to sing to me. I would tell them: listen. *All I want is to listen to you.*

But I would not attend the funerals. I would not eat another's grief, just as I would not gorge on another's sin. One I must number among my own, however, was that I often named another's as mine. And those, it is sad and also true, I ate.

I prised myself open and stuffed myself with guilt and borrowed burdens.

Sarala Kali was not beating her breasts when I first saw her. She was at the market, standing under a red tent, dividing fish and counting coins. Around her waist was a rope with a hundred keys attached to it. I had a camera around my neck and cicatrices all over my heart and soul. She lifted her eyes to where I waited, at the edge of the throng in front of her, and said her first words to me.

'Vanjaram?'

I shook my head. I did not want seer fish. And then the people in front of me eddied my vision and I could not see her any more.

## Sins

I went to Paris in a pre-apocalyptic summer. I took a room in Montmartre across from the Abbesses métro station with a window that looked on to a ficus-gilded wall. From here, I set out on my daily jaunts. Paris was the gift I gave myself when nobody would have me. In the Latin Quarter, I chanced on a singing woman with a marvellous mnemonic, an enormous cobalt parrot by her side; the next day they appeared right beside my hotel. One afternoon, I burst into tears in the Tuileries, unable to believe that in so vanquished a life I had bought myself this armistice of beauty. And then I crossed a bridge across the Seine and a Slavic woman stopped me in the street and told me I had dropped a gold ring. I had not, but it was mine from then on, at no cost but the sentimentality I had attached to it.

In Paris, I learnt that the words for 'fishers' and 'sinners' were the same, especially on my unnuanced tongue. I wrote them down in my notebook to share with Sarala Kali. *Pécheur. Pêcheur.* I wondered what she would say, and the wondering itself made me smile.

Sarala Kali spoke Tamil, English, Vagriboli and Telugu. She sang in the first, flirted in the second, traded in the third and swore in the last. Once, heavily drunk on sarayam, she told me she was the goddess of the spoken word and that she would bless me with a honeyed tongue. She was completely illiterate. My eyes were always full of tears.

**Tongue**

The first time Sarala Kali and I spoke properly, I had just been chased out of the partly senile but completely disarming Arcot Vanita's house, accused variously and in great aphoristic detail of stealing chickens, seducing her daughter-in-law and even driving a noisy used car. In truth, I had been there to give her prints of photographs taken at her great-great-grandson's ear-piercing ceremony the previous week. Sarala Kali was playing a mancala game on Arcot Vanita's neighbour's front porch, among a small crowd of women and children. 'What did she say to you?' she asked me. I told her. Sarala Kali nodded calmly.

'That bitch,' she said crisply in English, 'speaks as though she has seven-and-a-half sitting on her tongue.'

And I burst into laughter that drew sharp glances and mutters around us. Sarala Kali was smiling. I wanted to throw my arms around her.

'My name is Sarala Kali,' she told me. 'The next time you come, you will photograph me.'

From then on, I began to visit her in particular. I had first come to Ayodhyakuppam on a work assignment – a tedious one, which had required several visits. But it had ensnared me: I found it impossible to have looked upon so much grief and fortitude and then look away.

Even after the oppari singers had gotten to know me well, I could interact mostly only with women. Some lines cannot be crossed. Each woman I met was invariably the holder of some bereavement. A son who disappeared in the tsunami of 2004. A husband who killed himself because he could not bear that loss. A daughter who was burnt alive in the kitchen because she did not bring a dowry. Like menhirs outside of history, expected to outlast every event in their line of sight, they kept standing.

Sarala Kali was younger than the others, but as battle-broken. There were things that gave her away as an outsider – her facility for tongues, her uncanny self-possession, even her bluish skin that did not respond to turmeric, and those salamandrine eyes. Yet she belonged here, had staked the slum for her own and settled here. She carried a strange authority – I would see her selling fish and beating wet laundry like everyone else, but I would also see her being approached for loans, and I would see prepubescent boys run to the TASMAC to buy her liquor with notes she fished out of her blouse. From where she accrued this authority I do not know. There were pockets of her life into which she did not allow me.

The photographs were a ruse: they cost me nothing to shoot and were cheap to produce, and in this way I could keep returning to the kuppam, which gave me more than I was comfortable conceding. I wore my camera like a talisman, like I told a friend once. 'No, you wear it like a thaali,' she had said then. 'And this is your cardinal error.'

## The Battle

Some say the battle is easy, but the long years after it – bearing the memory of it like an internal scar – is the real wounding. I don't know this to be true. For me, a scar is proof of complex survival: not only of body and soul, but of tenderness itself. Tenderness as a way of being in the world.

For that alone, the battle is worth it.

Somewhere, there is a castle in which a lonely man banquets each night with a guest he meets by day in the wasteland, whom he reels in with a promise of undisguised or devious loneliness. That man is the Fisher King, whose realm wilts year by year because he has a wound that will not heal, and he has allowed it to overwhelm all that thrives. A sort of wild sexual jealousy. How the wound occurred to him is hard to say: sometimes a barb fired by a distant adversary is really of one's own hand. He leaves his abode only to cast a rod into water, and in this way he meets them: pilgrims, wayfarers, lost crusaders.

These travellers return with him for a night,

during which they feast with him, and as they do, they observe a marvellous and macabre procession. A sangreal chalice. A head on a platter, still uttering opinions. A lance fresh from slaughter. A sword cursed to shatter. And through this, that paper tiger waits silently for a single question from the observer, believing that this will set him free.

But why then did he maul the one who asked?

## Wound

The Fisher King was wounded in the groin, an injury so grave that it prevented him from leaving the ever-diminishing circles of his dominion. Until one day, all that existed for him were his castle and his river: one an inheritance, the other an unconquerable.

There is another kind of wounded soul.

Only the star-seers remember Chiron, the centaur whose groin too was pierced by a poisonous arrow. For nine days, he anointed the wound with herbs, but the venom completed its vise grip. A long and terrible endurance unto death for one who was a healer and teacher, who spent his life tending to the damage done to others. He could not heal himself, but oh, how he tried. Some of us do, you know. I think of you in your

chimeric empire and wonder how you can bear
to keep mirrors in it. Perhaps you think you have
outlived us, the maimed ones. Perhaps you have,
so simply, forgotten.

## Nepenthe

To survive you, I went to the very edge of
consciousness. And now, to live, I must erase the
memory of that erasure.

## The Fisher King

When the part of me that is married to darkness
met the part of you that was divorced from light, I
thought I had found the perfect chiaroscuro. All of
me that was luminous, all of you that was shadow,
all the parts and places that would not exist in the
absence of the other. What else is there to say but
this? I dove in. I drowned.

You surfaced on a farther shore. I never
surfaced at all.

And then you tugged at me, and all of me that
was hooked to you – which is to say, all of me –
came undone. Hook in my mouth, caught by the
throat, ensnared in the chakra of silence and voice.

When they told me you were the Fisher King I
was already a wraith in your empire of ruin. I was

already a naiad in your lake, waiting for you with watery eyes. And still you never looked at me. And still you never, ever heard me cry.

## Oppari

Widowhood is the first prerequisite. There are others: need, the strongest of them all. Nobody dares to profit from death unless she has truly lost everything. 'Of course my breasts hurt when I strike them,' one of the oppari singers told me once. 'But my belly hurts when I don't feed it.' In theory, that is all: to perform oppari you need only to be a widow who must make her living. It is inauspicious to say further, but it's impossible not to see the rest. Pathos and artistry. Passion and compassion.

Twice a month perhaps, news of a man's death. They would congregate immediately by the bridge by the Tiruvallikeni train station and make their way to the house of the bereaved. Krishna, Kodai, Siddhi and Sarala Kali.

The other three were elderly: a crone and two grandmothers. Only Sarala Kali seemed ageless, but there was something there I was not allowed to see. I would never learn the codes, but I could recognize their existence.

Something had shifted in my consciousness the

first time I watched them singing. In a room of mourning women, the widow was being stripped of her ornaments, and they sang as they broke her bangles, they sang as they unpinned the flowers from her hair and wiped the scarlet from her forehead, they sang of the beautiful yellow face she could no longer raise in public. And when they removed her nuptial chain, they wailed so wretchedly that it was as though every heartache that had rapiered through every life in history had awoken again as a single node of suffering. As they led her to the threshold of her door and she stepped across it, they handed a pall-bearer a clay pot of her ornaments. He would release them into the sea.

And then, everything crescendoed. The oppari singers formed a circle, facing inwards in a moving ring, and began to beat their breasts in rhythm, powerful and percussive. Palms striking flat and loud on chests, lungs wide open, their bodies turned to instruments, channelling pure unalloyed emotion.

'Ay ammaiadi,' chanted one.

'*Ay ammaiadi,*' followed the others.

'Ay appaiadi,' sang the leader.

'*Ay appaiadi,*' came the chorus.

The sight stirred me beyond expectation. Goosebumps broke out on my skin and I began to shiver. I had never seen anything so visceral. I held myself and wept as the corpse, a person I had never known even by name, was carried away.

By some understood rule, I always left Ayodhyakuppam by sunset, even on that first visit by assignment. But I know from hearsay what followed that night, and for sixteen nights after a cremation. Incineration is the work of men. The corpse winds its way, first to the sea and then through the city to the burning ground in the afternoon, accompanied by psychopompic dappan koothu dancers and their exultation of drums and flowers. Life is said to be sleepy, but death thrives with colour in Chennai. Funeral processions embroider its traffic jams with pomp and circumstance, and at night, the drumming continues for weeks. The men, stoned out of their sorrow, sing dirges. There are five types of gana, the songs that men fill the slums with on these nights: attu, aal, jigiri, deepa and marana. The first three deal with cinema, entertainment and intoxicants. Deepa refers to the light on the shore kept by those waiting for the fishing boats to return. Marana, of course, is for death.

The men only began to sing them in the last one hundred years. Women's lament is immeasurably ancient. On the sixteenth day, once more, they beat their breasts. Beyond that, all grief is personal.

Sarala Kali never told me the story of her widowing, but it was in the crescents that glinted in her eyes under streetlights sometimes, and in the words she used to love the dogs and cats that seemed to surround her at all times. It was in the timbre not of her oppari voice, but the one in which she sang thalattu. Lullabies. It was in the way her hands rested when empty, and in the hollow at her throat. Most of all, it was in the lies she told, the beautiful fictions, all the mythoi she channelled that could sound like they belonged to everyone. But those stories sprouted from her navel, and she tore them out like a lotus stalk so that she could feed the world in the myriad ways it came to her.

## Lagoon

A thousand or more years ago, my ancestors left the southern coasts of the peninsula to cast their fishing nets over the wide lagoons on the eastern promontory of the teardrop island. Their blood mingled with that of rulers who refused to prostrate even before deities in case their crowns fell from their heads, and grey-eyed spice brokers and bearers of the cross, and the extant and emigrant peoples of the south and north. It trickled through centuries and arrived finally in me – a moon perpetually in retrograde, with gravity in her eyes and the sea never out of her orbit.

In the braided veins of bloodmemory: surges, depths, lament, conchsong, salt and women's musk; the ocean always at the steps of one's door.

I arrived back on the island under a curse; unable to step into water because of an ailment of the lungs, banished, I looked at it without reprieve. From a tower on the shore with its back turned to the rising sun, I watched its lacustrine, tongue-tied sheen through night and day, and listened to the noise of a train that bit along the lip of the land at frequent intervals. There are superstitions about the crossing of water, and I learnt that every one of them was false.

On the farther border of the country, again the same malady. The closest I got to water was standing on a bridge and watching the anemone waving in the water below. There were armed men on that bridge, sigils of another war.

Of course I thought of you, even in that discognition. You had promised to take me home, to come back here with me, and it had never come to pass.

You said you could not leave your kingdom or your kind. And I could never belong to either one.

Still, I had come back – only, what good was

it to return in a warped time in which I myself was lost? I think of myself on the Kallady bridge, looking over its iron balustrades and not seeing its mermaids, not even seeing my own reflection.

But how vivid the pang of certain knowledge in the swoop of that sadness: that for you, I was this country itself – even if you could leave yours, you could never enter this place without the awareness of my absence by your side. I was your removed rib, your wounded thigh. But those are only the entities I used to be.

I forgive myself the fault of having fallen into you. I give myself back to me with a correction of narratives. You were a canard. I was a myth. A mermaid, a fisherwife, a selkie of the southern sphere. Throwing her net out as though she meant to entangle the stars, when all along she had what she wanted – or what she wanted could never be had. She was only fishing the night.

**Lullaby**

*Aararo, aariraro…*

**Mermaid**

Until the civil war, the mermaid was not a legend. On full moon nights, you could pay your fare and step into a fisherman's boat and he would take you into the lagoon. And you could keep the flat end of your oar in the water and hold its handle to the mollusk of your ear and listen to her sing.

Maybe there was only one mermaid, maybe a commonwealth. Maybe mermen. Maybe more.

And then for thirty years it was no longer safe to venture out at night. You could be a saboteur, you could try to blow up the bridge, you could engage in any kind of criminal activity under the protections of darkness, or – most of all – you could be disappeared. It was no longer so simple, the act of listening. And so the mermaid of Batticaloa became its singing fish, became its symbol – shaped into tacky plaster statues and printed into menu logos and placed in the most shallow of regards.

Some say the serenade – that sound that could be an orchestra of strings and keys, or the resonance of a pulsar, or the seduction of a fingertip on a wine glass – comes from the inhabitants of conus shells. Some say the singing comes from frogs. Some say, at least in secret, that there surely must still be mermaids in those waters.

You could not listen to the song when the military had control of the bridge. For thirty years, she must have sung only for herself. So that when finally we ventured back into the water, it was us and not her who had perhaps been forgotten.

Now, for now anyway, you can still hear it. On a full moon night, the kind under which my grandmother would chase and catch scuttling crabs on the beach with no necessity for artificial light, I could ask someone to take me into the Batticaloa lagoon in his boat. And if I listened very closely, over the traffic and the ambient noise and the world as it has now become, I could hear it. The singing.

## Shipwreck

At the entrance of the church of the saint of lost things, climbing out of a taxi on the morning after a star-crossed wedding, my uncle told me an origin story.

He said: 'A long time ago, a Portuguese ship was wrecked by a cyclone on this shore. But the captain and crew made it alive, and staggering on to dry land they found a shrine to Kali. In gratitude for their rescue, they threw the idol into the sea and instated this church.'

'So that's why it's so powerful,' I said. All things are palimpsests; nothing wasted, nothing forgotten, nothing without counterweight or compensation. We never have the whole story. We are reincarnated in the midst of narratives, making reparations for the sins of stories past.

We queued to reach the altar of St. Anthony, patron saint of what is lost. I tried to count the things I could pray to have given back to me when I noticed the words on either side of the crucifix at the centre of the church:

Priest          Victim

Perhaps they were the same thing. Perhaps one fed off the other, and the other off the one. Two ways to tell the story of what happened to you, and what happened to me because of it. You were alone. You wanted to be alone. You were wanted. You, alone.

But when we arrived at last before St Anthony, even your name fled from my memory. For the first time in what could have been a long time I could not think of a single thing I had lost that had not been returned to me in a hundred shimmeringly beautiful fragments.

## Apocrypha

I could never confirm the apocrypha, but this is what I know: in that church in Kotahena, I also stood, with my palms in the gesture of pleading, at the feet of the mother of god, and whether she was Mother or God mattered not. In the moment of surrender, we close our eyes.

## Heart/Beat

Ay ammaiadi *(ay ammaiadi)*, ay appaiadi *(ay appaiadi)*.

## Pledge

For six weeks, I carried a lock around Europe, neither needing it nor knowing why. A tiny lock, one that could easily break, whether or not I chose to use it. I don't even know how it got into my bags, but one day I reached into a pocket and it was there. And I kept it because it was a spare, and I was a woman on my own, and sometimes we are driven by a logic not of personal habit or making.

Then one day in Paris, I crossed the Seine and around me on either side were locks, thousands of locks, all along the grates on the balustrades of the bridge. There were names on them, and simple hearts, and although I would not be able to ask what this rite meant until after I had completed it, I knew immediately why I had carried that little lock with me through four countries.

I wrote my name, only mine, and clicked the lock closed, and then I threw the key into the river.

And then I crossed over to the other side.

## Tributary

Eventually, and not so long afterwards at all, I did learn how to love myself. And a few years later, when the city of Paris unclasped the weight of all those locks, I breathed a sigh of relief. I was mine again, I was mine, and I was ready to belong to someone else, too.

But that summer, and for a miasma of time that surrounded it, I struggled with the knowledge of deep loathing, betrayals, permanent excisions. You were not the only one who sought to destroy me that year. Somebody who never knew you once assured me that your guilt was to be your entire life, and if this is true, let me tell you: forgive your lovelessness. I have already forgiven you.

There were other things that I almost died of. But so I would not die of silence, I opened my maw sometimes and let a primal cry slip free. And when even that was not affordable to me, I inked lines into my body and washed them away in salty water.

That was immediate relief. Indulgence would come later – handwritten cantos in handmade notebooks too pretty to expend on anything less elegant than slow and unredeemable ruin.

## Après Toi

What a shame I was still in love
with you in Paris, settling my sadness
on the steps of Sacré-Cœur, all the beauty
in the fathomable world before me
and not a breath in my body
that wasn't your name.

## Ave Maria

In the end, the only stories that loving you brought me were the stories of what it meant to not be loved by you. There was a little church I didn't enter in Paris, beside my hotel. But I would sit on a bench across from its entrance and read and daydream as the city's centripetal life force waltzed around me in that sweetly decaying summer. One evening, I sensed someone watching me and raised my eyes slowly. His white hair was cropped close, and he was walking alone, a slight arrhythm to his gait. Handsome, local. I smiled, and so did he. And then, just as slowly, I tilted my chin back down to my book again. He was only walking past. He had such kind eyes.

You can give yourself a city if you love the whole world. You can give yourself the ocean if you take the risk of drowning. You can give yourself the love story you deserve, if you write it yourself, if you let the ink itself become your life.

I never forgot that gesture – the exchange of smiles in front of that church. How beautiful self-containment is. A moment like a red umbrella in the rain, under which a whole world proceeds.

## She, of the Sea

Somewhere in the rich semibreve of this life, I will go back to France. I will walk the Tuileries in winter and gaze at the Eiffel Tower through the barren and beautiful trees, wrapped in soft wool and self-knowledge. And at the end of the month of May, I will go to the south of the country and enter the belly of the Earth, and bow to Her in the underground grotto in which She is worshipped. I will make a candle tree of my petitions, a rosary of my gratitude.

Gypsy queen, goddess of perdurance.

Sara-la-Kali, Sara e Kali, Sati-Sara.

And having worshipped at her altar, in Saintes-Maries-de-la-Mer, I will join the procession that takes her idol out on to the streets, above ground, and then to the ocean from which she came, or by which she wandered, keeping vigil, her eyes trained on the horizon for the exiles who would set their bloodline to root on this shore. Whose story did you ask for? The tellers, the takers, the traumatizers or the torch-bearers? Each of them is stigmata, each is its own evidence.

I've watched from a distance for a long time, small and dark. And I know that somewhere in the long purview of all that will come to pass, there already exists a portrait of me, with my hands full of roses, a speck in a crowd of raised palms, watching the goddess on her palanquin flanked by white horses knee-deep in the tides. And I am squinting through sunlight to see her, my lips murmuring in prayer.

Mother of many names. Mother of the honeyed tongue. Mother of the never-not-broken.

She, of the sea.

## Conchology

What I want is a beloved – to *be* beloved – someone who knows me the way the conch knows the sea, holding me in the rush of their own blood. The lovers I have had, however many or few, knew me only in whorls and whispers. I slipped my tongue into their ears and they sipped from the shell of me. None of them heard me. None of them listened.

## Lines

Once, I heard a historian remark at a conference that what set apart the Greek epics from the South Asian ones was their immutability. The Odyssey could take place only as was written. But sung and improvised and appropriated and forgotten, there were hundreds of Ramayanas. How I told the story of us varied based on whether I was under siege, under a spell, or under a heartbreak of a harvest moon.

For a rondure of seasons, you were the only thing I talked about.

'If he liked it, he should have put a lakshman-rekha around it,' shrugged Sarala Kali one night in Ayodhyakuppam, watching me pour more vodka into a plastic bottle of lime soda. I was sobbing, moving around her kitchen while somewhere in the near distance firecrackers – a wake? a cricket match? – were going off like drunken punctuations.

'Really? Is it that simple?'

'It is that simple. You wanted him to set the

parameters. What broke you is that he refused to concede they existed, and then punished you for stepping across them.'

'He—'

'No. You. You.' She pointed at me. 'He may have pushed your finger into the earth, he may have pushed you bodily even, but it was you who drew the line. Be brave. A day will come when you will not look back. Until then, keep walking.'

'And what do I do? What do I do as I keep walking?'

'This. This will do.'

## Crossing

There is a bridge that those like me cross, and having crossed it, can never negotiate again. You were the point of no return for me. Because I could not bear to walk away from you, I let you leave, and when you turned around, I turned away. I saw a crown of compassion, a burden. Beyond that, all was burning.

## Burning

Sarala Kali took me to the burning ground once. Don't ask me anything further. The universe is a ghat is a stage is the heart.

## Refuge

There is no country the shape of what you have lost.

## Wing Mirror

Sarala Kali's disappearance stunned everyone who knew her into a particular kind of silence. It was as though it was easiest of all to behave as though she had never existed, had never brandished the banner of her big laugh or cast her cowries in the kuppam. Had never been there, and so had never no longer been there, her front door wide open and her kitchen intact but not a scrap of her presence left in the building.

What they will tell you is that, after that, I stopped visiting them. The truth as I know it is that they closed their ranks against me. I had brought too much of the outside with me, and with it too many questions. There was a whiff of rumour about what I might have taken. At the Zam Bazaar police station, they finally let me go at 11.35 p.m. on that clear and cold December night and I swallowed my salty tears outside the gate as I waited for my friend to pick me up. I had eaten nothing since that morning, had been spoken to by no one who wasn't in regulation khaki. There was a contusion on my wrist from where I had crashed into a wing mirror when someone – a man – had shoved me before the police came. My bangles too had broken then. My friend arrived in his car and reached over to unlock the door, then ran over to my side when he saw me struggling to open it. He took me straight to his house and fed me buttered toast and tea. In the morning, he drove me home. They said: there would be nothing on my permanent record.

This is what I took: nothing, everything, all I could carry.

Nobody ever asked what it took out of me.

## Tails

I'll never forget the first time I made Sarala Kali laugh. She was bringing her cleaver down upon a multitude of heads: chopping fresh red snapper and imported basa ('nothing as boring as basa,' my friends who have never set foot in a fish market rue in restaurants, and I smile even more ruefully) for a big order. A catering gig; she had a connection with someone who'd do the cooking, and someone else who'd do the delivery. She was working on her front porch because it was a sweetly sunless day, and in this way she would miss none of the conversation on the street.

It must have been the third time or so that I visited her, after my unceremonious ousting from Arcot Vanita's house. The first time, Sarala Kali netted my life's history over betel leaf bhajji and sun-dried prawns. The second time, I accompanied her to a political rally on the beach. The third time, I had come determined to take her photograph. She was so lovely in that rose-light, that late morning in the slum by the sea.

'What a pity you're so clever, when all the boys you like are as brainless' – *tak tak, sadhak sadhak* – 'as these fish' – she swept a red-queenly carnage of heads off the porch and into a gaping garbage bin – 'that *I* have the wonderful headwriting of having to meet.'

'Yes, well,' I said tartly, 'God gave me an exceptionally beautiful mind to match my exceptionally beautiful behind.' And when she dropped her blade and pressed her hand to her chest and almost wheezed in delight, I might not have been prouder of anything else I'd done in – oh I don't know, a year?

I want to say that I have a photograph. But I don't.

# Smell

In Tiruvallikeni, there is a famous temple to the god who holds a conch in one hand, and a discus in another. With one, dismembering. With the other, remembering. In this transmogrified life of mine, I go there sometimes – hair scented by fresh jasmine, my arms full of holy basil. Whole worlds span between the temple and the slum. Did Matsyagandha ever feel like a fraud, after the smell of fish was taken away from her skin? I can never go back to Ayodhyakuppam, but this is as close as I come – sandal paste and vermilion on my forehead, making my quiet way from the temple to the beach, memory raw like the odour of blood and salt in the ocean wind.

## CORVUS

When we went to lunch the day before the moon turned into a white crow, I slid a foot out of its slipper and found his toes with it. We were at a Chinese restaurant neither of us had been to before, a place I think was called Sunflower; or maybe that was the name of the parlour beside it, with its posters of Shanghainese beauties from another era in the window and hanzi characters above its entrance. I sat facing the door, which opened rarely. The restaurant comforted me, its small red altar in a corner some sigil of what was real amongst its own exaggerations.

The bottom of my belly thrummed pleasantly, sated and hungry at once. Kāma examined the menu.

'How do you say "thank you" in Chinese?'

'Xie xie.' In those days I took pleasure in knowing I could thank, swear and say 'I love you'

in a handful of languages – everything I thought
I needed for at least one affair in a foreign land.

But he spoke to me mostly in Tamil, and I
spoke to him mostly in English, and in bed the two
merged: the latter for commands, jokes, smut. The
former, always, for tenderness.

The waiter came and took our order. Kāma
handed the menu back to him and said gravely,
'Xie xie.'

I broke into a laugh, aghast. He looked at me
and I looked at him and I shook my head but
couldn't look away. I had let him get away with
worse.

The food arrived and we disengaged our toes at
the same moment. He scooped the fried rice on to
my plate. I carved a portion of the Mandarin fish
for him. I wiped two sets of cutlery with a tissue
and handed his to him, feeling a pang of regret that
I had never learnt how to use chopsticks, which
an ex-boyfriend had called elegant. I watched him
begin unhesitatingly, without waiting for me, and
once again the question of what drew him to me
more flickered in my mind briefly: the glamorous
patchwork of my history or the simple fact of my
face, its unambiguous nativity.

I had known him for a much longer time than
I had been sleeping with him, but sex has a way

of setting back the clock. Everything before those few months had faded into irrelevance. He had re-entered my life like a changing season: without omen, a single door opened on to a transformed landscape, rainfall from a cloudless sky, a tree that burst into ripeness overnight. I prepared for him to leave it the same way.

What drew me to him was the same thing that has ever drawn me to any man, before or since: a latent brutality, an undisclosed yet evident vulnerability. An instinct for self-preservation, and the willingness to allow its breaching. The ability to deepen my capacity for all of these in equal measure.

~

Someone once told me about the sadness, a long time ago, before I would have imagined that sadness possible.

He said: 'It will begin, as will all else that will follow it, already tinged with a sadness you won't know what to do with.'

I thought he had meant the sadness of the past, the sadness that I would enter a new entanglement – and all others that would follow it – carrying. But what he had meant, I understood eventually, was only the sadness of foreknowledge. Of seeing an end before it happened. Of standing at a window and looking at the sea sparkling in the afternoon sun, while inside your body something far less pacific shattered itself over and over, a tide you had come to know, recognize, call by name.

Because the man who had told me this had been neither among my lovers nor among my regrets, I could accept his words without introspection, the way one carries the fact of one's childhood, or one's own name. I thought of them often the season I was with Kamalesh. I would uncoil his arms from around me and go and sit at his window while he took his afternoon nap, and I would ponder those words, ponder that sadness.

It was always the same those afternoons. The leafless tree in the empty lot beside the apartment block would sway lightly in the breeze. The sea would darken. A murder of crows would flap their dark wings low across the sky. And I would think, already nostalgic, that this was what I would miss – the sound of waves and the cawing, that particular beach wind, the sense of being at a boundary and at a beginning all at once. I would go to his window so that I would always remember to keep the horizon in my sight, its approaching peril, its open, guileless face.

Kāma, he liked me to call him. The god of love expressed through lust. It wasn't the name his parents had given him. But it wasn't for either of us to question.

He would pick me up in his Maruti 800 from the back entrance of the Marundeeswarar temple, which I'd walk to from the bus depot at Thiruvanmiyur. We would make love through the morning, and then we'd cook or go out for lunch. This was our routine, almost every other day, for months. I could have spent all my life that way, but the beauty of those present things was that they belonged only to their moment, their succinct and singular tempo.

~

We had parked right outside the restaurant. At the far end of the road was the church of the Virgin of Vailankanni, and beyond that, the sea. It had not yet rained that year, and wouldn't for months more, but this part of the city didn't have the same suffocating quality the heat gave the rest. That would change, of course, once the neighbourhood had been thoroughly layered with his prints. I was trying to avert this. Emotional geography collects like plaque: a little carelessness and it's there before you know it. He put his sunglasses on and looked at me. I smiled. He thought he was very sexy with his shades on. He was.

'My car needs to be washed,' he murmured apologetically, and pointed at the crow shit. I hadn't even noticed. There was a lot of it, even on the front window. I had never noticed, though it now seemed clear from the dust that coated the rest of it that I must have seen his car dozens of times since he had last had it cleaned.

'Your ancestors are shitting all over your intentions,' I said, not meaning it at all.

'And yours?' He cocked an eyebrow. Sometimes I wondered why my parents had ever left Madras when, decades later, my life was an '80s Tamil film anyway, all kissing on rooftops and curfews and the way P. Susheela's voice rose with unhindered clarity from the watchman's mini-radio downstairs during the scheduled power cuts.

Back in his flat, we spent the next two hours laughing and cuddling, with him insisting he was going to sleep, but always catching himself before he actually did. 'It's good to hold you,' he breathed into my ear. And although I knew better, I couldn't help but recognize that what he meant was: he would rather hold me halfway, half-awake, and know it than slumber not mindful that I was in his arms at all.

~

That night I woke up feeling like I was weightless in water, like the sea had come in through my doors and cradled me in my sleep. I let it lull me back to sleep. When I woke up for a second time, it was 3.30 a.m. Outside my window the sky was tenebrous, reddish. The silhouette of palm fronds wavered in the wind through the wrought-iron bars. I was thirsty. I was miles from the beach and I longed for it. I wondered if Kāma could hear the tides from his bed, if I would still be awake if I was there too.

There were crows cawing even at that hour. I got up and retied my lungi, washed my face, poured myself a small glass of cranberry juice and wished there was some vodka in it. I checked my messages. A friend on the other side of the world had recorded Szymborska into his phone, and I listened to his grave and earnest reading against the landscape of what I knew of his loss and what I knew of my longing, and I wasn't certain what lines to send him, to travel back to him by way of thanks and consolation.

There was no sense in going back to bed, not when the night had coaxed me awake so many times, as if to say, like a ravenous lover, *I belong to you alone*. I watched the sunrise bleed over the sky and when my mother came out from the bathroom, her wet hair turbaned, and touched my shoulder and said, 'It's Saturday, will you keep the rice out?' I put on my slippers and went downstairs. On the stone wall at the back of the property, I placed the handful of boiled rice and mustard seeds she had given me, stepped away, and waited for the first black bird to swoop down.

~

Because my grandmother's funeral had been on a Saturday, a small black chicken was tied by its feet to the front of her bier. As a woman I had not been allowed into the cremation grounds; I can only surmise that it would have burnt with her on her pyre, alive but comatose. It wasn't comatose when I knelt before her pyre though. I had placed my forehead on the cement in our driveway and closed my eyes to its squawking.

I walked back down the same driveway and went back up to our flat, listening to the sounds of the crows behind me. We had started to feed the ancestors only after my grandmother had died. That was a love that was worth generations.

Asclepius, whose mother Coronis was betrayed by a crow, was carved out of his mother's womb as she lay on her pyre. His name meant 'to cut open'. He became the god of healing. His father, Apollo, had had so many lovers – yet he had not been able to fathom the idea that he was not Coronis' only one.

When I lay in Kāma's arms I had neither wounds nor memory of them. Only the sadness, sometimes. He was the only one who ever adored me. To adore is to worship, without fear or plea. For this and no other reason, he has my loyalty for life.

~

Much as well as a little later, there would be men who mimed those gestures of intimacy that only Kāma, I believed, ever rendered sincerely. And as much as I loved, or wanted to love them, it wasn't the same – no one else stroked my hair that way or held my feet that way or eyed me across a room quite like he did. No one else didn't know how to lie.

There was one man who seemed to discover

the eloquence of kissing the hand only when I first kissed his, because the way he then took mine and did the same suggested unfamiliarity, wonder, the simplicity of imitation. I would later grieve thinking about the other women he would confer the same upon, this tenderness I had given him. As though anything in any of us is truly new, unclaimed.

That was Martand. From him I learnt the pleasure of the licked eyelid, what it means to paint the eye with the salt of the tongue. I, too, would give that gesture away, to an intoxicated lover who kissed even my elbows as we fell asleep, only to tell me the next day that he had no memory of having initiated the encounter between us. I said nothing. How do we do this – speak with our bodies even as we swallow our voices?

The crow that betrayed Coronis was scorched by the very one he betrayed her to. Its snowlike feathers turned obsidian. Silence is its own terrible smoulder. But truth-telling lacquers a darker, richer damage.

I betrayed Martand with Kāma. Neither of them will tell you what I did. Both of them will tell you it didn't matter. But only I know what it cost me. Only I knew that incineration.

~

Kāma, the god of desire, was also incinerated.

All things are written. The gods already knew that only the son of the meditating Shivan could kill the asura who wreaked havoc on their rites. A son with a warrior's temperament and six perfect jewel-like faces. But Shivan was an ascetic, a widower, turned inwards through the falconry hood of contemplation. His wife, Dakshayani, had immolated herself. Inconsolable, Shivan had lifted her charred body to his shoulder and tried to obliterate his consciousness – obliterate the universe – in dance. Unable to witness his unbearable suffering, the other gods had her body dismembered – each fragment of flesh and drop of blood hallowing the earth where it fell. Every sacred space begins as a theatre of grief. Out of trauma comes transformation.

The dismembered goddess was reborn: comely, wiser, her heart cleansed by a different lifetime of tears, she laughed more freely and lived more fiercely. She was a deepened furrow. Emancipated this time from shame and obligation, having seen beyond the illusion of that which binds into the truth of that which is, she longed to once again be Shivan's companion. And the gods longed for the son she would then bring into being. And so she stood there before Shivan in her dancing anklets, her pulse thrumming even in her throat, and watched as Kāma, parrot-rider, manifested an untimely spring in the cosmos. He moved in the spiral of a southern breeze, a hum of fragrant sweetness. He poised an arrow of flowers strung on a bow of sugarcane and took aim at the meditating god.

At the moment of piercing, a furious Shivan opened his third eye and the fire of his wrath turned Kāma to ashes instantly.

And then he noticed Parvati, her turmeric limbs and luminescent eyes.

For his righteous intent, for the six-faceted son and the consort of variegated personae, for love itself, in its manifold dimensions, Kāma was revived. He was allowed to prevail. But formlessly.

Which is why the spirit of love is bodiless; only its performance is corporeal.

At that time, in those days when I would thirst for the sea because something was always burning, Kāma was my only lover. I was not his only girlfriend, though. She was nowhere in the vicinity, not truly, that other woman on a distant continent. We said her name between us sometimes in conversation, in order to put distance between ourselves.

Not long after it was over with Martand,

Kāma and I went to the beach on a new moon night. Valmiki Nagar. The ocean sulking, holding her secrets closer than usual. We sat on the shore and he let me cry, holding my hand as I did. An aravani came to us and clapped in Kāma's face for the rupee notes he promptly fished out of his breast pocket.

'You've come with your girl, mapillai,' she said. 'Don't you want a good long life together?' She thought we were newly-weds. I giggled. In less than three years, he would be someone else's husband. I was sure I was not meant to be anybody's bride.

~

The sighting of a white crow is said, I would learn later on, to be an omen of a blessing that would come to be lost through greed. The white crow says: *Look within*. The white crow says: *See, ahead, what you will be without*.

I rarely spent the night at Kāma's. It was too difficult to do often – the question of what I would tell my parents was one worth risking only with discretion. In my twenties and for a long time afterwards, the city was still that sort of place. This didn't mean it never happened. The first time I slept over had been impulsive: there are moons over Madras sometimes that eclipse everything else, all semblance of pretence or pragmatism. There had been one such moon that night, orange-flamed and balsamic. There had been no question of going home.

That Saturday, however, as I took the lift back up to the apartment after feeding the ancestors, there was a definite whirr of plan-making in my mind. I intended to spend the weekend with him, to arrive a little before sunset and stay until after dinner the following evening. Somewhere there was a suggestion of a long drive, later that day or the following morning. We would trace the hem of the sea southwards, from his house on the border of the city to as far as we felt we could go without losing ourselves.

And then we would park the car in some semi-private enclave, behind a stone wall someone built to stake and divide land, and run into one of the hundred casuarina groves, through the trees, not stopping until our feet were in the water and our heads were in the clouds.

~

The casuarina beach was somewhere between the artists' village and the temple of the eternal bridegroom. We had done this enough times before: turning off the road when the desire seized us. Always a different beach along the coast. We were not always alone – in the near distance we could usually see others like us, pairs and sometimes small groups. We veered away from loners. They always scared us back to the car in some uninterrogated anxiety.

It was a full moon night: a perfect moon, gravid and gorgeous, already high enough in the sky to be an immaculate alabaster circle.

'In my mother's country,' I said, 'days of the full moon are public holidays.'

He kissed my hand as we stepped into the water. 'When are we going there?' he asked, and I smiled at the moon because I'd already given away too much.

~

How small a crow can seem when it is still and how large when it takes flight towards you.

The moon was a coin. The moon was a compass rose. The moon was a crow: quickfire light, quills of ivory. She swooped right down towards us, mouth open, pink as modesty. Grandmother eyes. Primordial voice.

We'd been holding hands, lying on our backs with our feet in the foam and our hair full of drying sand. We both leapt up, gasping. We'd seen it, feathered like salt, heard that unmistakable cry. But when we looked up again, the words desiccating on our tongues, there she still was. Calmly unblinking, still brooched to the sky. Not a wisp of a feather, not an echo. Occulted moon, more enigmatic than ever before.

~

Because we had both seen it, neither one could correct the other, could say: trick of the light, trompe l'œil. Kāma was quiet on the drive back. It was I who, in the absence of all other sound, filled it with singing.

~

For a while, we were lucky. For a while, we were happy.

Beautiful Kāma, with his godlike body and his childlike folly. Beautiful Kāma who set all the rules he thought he lived beyond. Who tested the waters not knowing—poor baby—that water is volatile. That you cannot measure a depth. You can only measure a distance.

~

At the time, it had ended painlessly enough. I had walked away from that apartment, with its sea view and its sun-cartridged afternoons, and hailed an auto – I will never forget this – driven by a man who wore a pendant around his neck that was shaped like the skeleton of a fish.

Most of the pain, that sadness that had tinged everything (I came to realize later), had been in the effort of keeping it from meeting its denouement, but once I allowed it to happen it slipped away cleanly, without residual rawness. Amputation is simple, a question of the correct knife. Resurrection requires more subtle energies.

I would return to that apartment in so many guises. Adulterous, armed to the teeth, my body an arcana of alibis. I don't know what it is about infidelity that makes it so damn *hot*. I don't know how it was ever worth it. No, that is not true. The problem is that, in my most profoundly honest moments, naked of spirit and windswept of heart, I do.

But that evening, wilful and self-possessed, I walked out believing it was over, that I had seen the last of those seaward windows. They *were* over, those days of rhythmically uncomplicated pleasure. What I didn't know was that there would still be other kinds. Of complications. Of pleasures. I took flight with such certitude.

And like a winged creature blotting itself out on to the sun, I scorched right into Martand.

~

The one thing I know to be true is not that love is all there is, or that everything dies. It is that everybody has *want*. It's a tiny nerve, a vein of gypsum, that runs through everything – everyone – and sometimes I see someone else's so clearly that it catches me by the throat. In every place I have been in the world I have looked at people and seen right through into their lives, into the one true thing for which this wretched bittersweet is worth enduring, and I have broken into pieces at the recognition of it. It's the smallest thing. The smallest, smallest, smallest thing.

~

Kāma brings his children to me for my foreign folk tales and the seer fish curry I must stop making for them when they become old enough to decipher the recipe from taste. The boy comes up to my hip, the place on my body where a phoenix would be inked on to my skin, if I were capable of that kind of lifelong allegiance. The girl, like her father, presses herself to my breast when she hugs me, and always needs to be coaxed to let go.

~

It is astonishing how strong you become, when you've spent a lot of time being other people's weaknesses. I could never find the kind of responsible love that most people had, if they had it at all. I fell hopelessly for maladroit men who took the 'cage' in 'ribcage' to heart, and admired women who had never known what long-married love was like. I was always the object of desire, the souvenir, the receptacle of memories of wildness, a parenthesis in their experience of an unexceptional world.

Because I could not find slow love, love that could age, I grew into the evanescence that others sought me for. After a point, I could no longer withhold – and I could no longer amputate. So I began to adore simply, not loudly, and always in the awareness that those like me must live like flowering trees. We are who we are, prosperously or otherwise. And our lives are crowned, now and then, with moments of exaltation – each held and breathed in deeply, and then let go.

Some nights I still wake to the sound of crows crying. And I think of Kakabhujandi, the raven in the tree of life, who listens to the ancient stories and tells them again. Always adding his watermark, his song that is also the first syllable in the old alphabet – ka. The same word as the question – Why?

And depending on where I am, I will stay in bed and look at the bruise-bitten night through the skylight or the undraped window. Always, this sky. And I'll sigh, calm my breath and listen, and wonder.

*Why why why*

## STONE

It took my breath away to find out you were made of stone. I thought I knew them; I took them into my life as cairns of pleasure and protection: silver-soldered turquoise that chandeliered from my ears, talismans of carnelian and rose quartz, jade trinkets, pebbles from places I wanted to keep carrying, even a fragment of perfectly chthonic obsidian, an object of wonder. Once, when you were less petrified, I gifted you an amethyst. A single gemstone, so small it could not have caught the light even if we had riveted it to a carousel of mirrors. It was for you to drop into liquor. I wanted to detoxify your life of all that poisons it.

So, stone. When I held your arms as you held your weight over mine, you were not stone. You were fresh blood and spellbound breath and cardinally human. You were forgiven for a thousand impossible years. You were neither sinner nor sin. I raised my eyes and you were the canvas of Lascaux, constellated with maps.

And so the mystery of your resistance was an endless cave. I could catch no light within it, no matter how devoutly I cast my dowsing rod. Some time after all had calcified, in the long overwinter when all that had happened between us became no more than igneous memory, I held the word in my palm again and considered its uncharted possibilities. They told me it was a giver's word, a word that at once meant withholding and worship, a word that meant not coldness but compassion. They told me not to apply it to your cowardice, not to name you bijou and wreck myself again on your rocks. But whose tenderness was it, then – yours or mine – that left me gasping, unravelled by narrative? One word, and I held the story of you like a lapidary. And once again my desire was oxblood and ochre, a hurricane of wild horses, your enigma summoned before me like a revelation, an omphalos tendrilled with honeybees.

## SWEET

They say that if you dream of the one you long for on a night when you have kept four lotus petals under your pillow, your love has not gone unreciprocated. In the French Quarter I see them, all pale formality and long-stemmed leaning, and smile remembering this. I have no use for the sad dignity of lotuses, not here. Tonight, in the other city, I will sleep alone for the first time in weeks, but this is how it works: while I am here, this is all there is. Nothing exists beyond the periphery of desire.

We have stopped for petrol and for gerberas, my weakness. Through the window, I pick and point out a crimson one, for comeliness, and a salmon one, for greed, and the man who sells them out of bright plastic buckets smiles into my eyes as he hands them to me through the window, a cat's cradle of wet stalks and silken petals. Yesterday, someone tenderly lifted an eyelash from my cheek, held her fingertip near my lips and told me to make a wish as I blew it away. 'I have everything I want this morning,' I laughed, and I meant it. My bare feet were in cool sepia earth, soft with recent rain, and above us the neem trees were susurrus with applause and coincidence. 'Then wish for more mornings like this,' she said, and I kissed her wrist and did.

I wait in the taxi and watch you pace the cobblestones, impatient. You are going to the city for work, a date, obligations, curiosities. I am going to the city because that is where I stay, enduring years like these for days like the ones that have just passed. There is salt in the wind, and my wounds, though dulcified, are still wrought delicate.

The driver has disappeared. 'If you get out of that car, honeybee, you will run away too,' you complain. 'So stay inside.' I imagine stepping out, refusing to leave, escaping to the village to live like a poet, a potter, raising papaya saplings and children mud-luscious and illegitimate, coming to town twice a week to wander these streets of Pondicherry ochre and Virgin Mary blue. 'I know you, madcap,' you say, reaching a hand into the window to smooth back my hair. And you do.

But there's only so long I can sit inside; already

the heat and the weight of departure have begun to vex. You concede, open the door with a flourish, and I tumble out with a mismatched flower behind each ear and my heart heavy as a skirt worn in the sea.

I lean into your chest and you hiss fiercely into my hair, 'And what else do you have to do in that city but cry? So save it. You're still here.'

And just then, the driver appears at the far end of the street, carrying a clear bag of white nectarines in one hand and one of swimming goldfish in the other, glitter-glorious in the sunlight. We both notice him, and at once, the perfect circuitry of a single thought occurs. 'Do you remember that afternoon when we were riding back home on the bike and at the start of the Dindivanam highway –'

'– when they had just chopped down all those trees and we were shattered to see them standing there like amputees –'

'– but on our right, to the east, was the translucent full moon, and to our left, on the west –'

'– the sun, perfectly parallel, two heavenly bodies in the sky with us right in the middle.'

You smile.

'It was 3.30 p.m. on one of the first days of that year.' I shake my head. 'I'll never forget it.'

You open the door and whisper, 'For you, always, the sun, the moon, the stars.'

'For my sister's children in Chennai,' grins the driver, apologetic. He places the fish and fruit in the passenger seat, and we're in the back, doors locked before we can regret it.

'That's where we're going,' you say, and nod slowly.

When we pass the junction that leads back to the village, I will blow a kiss in its direction and bless the memory of that dusk, beautiful and bloodshot, when I was overwhelmed with love for the land that gave rise to the dirt road on which a girl I had met just that morning and I had braked our motorbike because a peacock had darted across, right to left, and moved amidst the undergrowth while we – stunned speechless – watched.

So let me ride back with you in this taxi you have hired so we can talk or hold hands all the way up the east coast to the other city, where we will separate because magic this pure cannot suffer a place like that. We are not there yet. But as we pierce its limits, you will get out of the car without saying goodbye. Alone again, I will re-enter the city concealed like a mercenary, the weeks I have spent at home already fading, like a dream too surreal to hold whole, too sweet to bear. It will be months before we meet again, almost as long before we speak. In the car we will have been mostly silent, each lost in thoughts that isolate the other; as if in preparation.

And even when there's nothing to look at in the hours ahead but other cars verging towards or away from the holiest place we know, there, reflected in the windshield: a mirage of marigold, fish swirling in the sky in a trick of the light.

You won't put your arms around me when we part, and I won't promise you a thing or pretend to know what is true, except that life is long and love is small and selfish and I do love you, I love you, I do.

## MOTHER-TONGUED

The first time I spent the night at the cunning linguist's, a blood orange moon rose out of the sea. We watched it ascend from his third-floor window and later, when we both woke momentarily mid-sleep, he grabbed my chin and said 'Yennadi?' and kissed me rough-soft. That was the moment of my downfall. When I turned up at his doorstep the next time wearing – by sheer coincidence – a sari, he made love to me without taking it off. When I ran away to Auroville (crying all the way down on the AC bus from Koyambedu), he called within a week to say, 'Nee Pondicherry-le irukira nerathila, Madras-ay kamathila vaadi poghuthu.'

'You are in Pondicherry, and all of Chennai is wilting with desire,' I explained to friends who did not understand. Flush with superlative sex and

80

dizzy with delusion, I told everyone I knew. But translation only went so far.

When he fucked me, I spoke in tongues and in terrible clichés. Mostly, though, I made love in my mother-tongue. I hung from it like it was a ladder thrown over a ledge.

He would disappear for weeks, once for as long as two months, and then he would call again. He had a way of resurfacing that erased both the fact and the length of his absence. He would show up with his arms full of allurements, conjuring himself out of thin air, with a tantara and a terrible gleam in his eye. He would say, 'Vaa-di yen raasathi.' *Come here, my little queen.* And I would go. I would slip into lace panties, pull a garter belt up to my thigh under the layers of a petticoat and an '80s-printed sari, spritz rosewater between my breasts, and go.

## GIGOLO MAAMI

He was the perfect wife. When we were done screwing without taking off the saris he loved so much on me, he would press a fresh erection against my bum and refold the pleats neatly, looking over my shoulder while I swooned in his arms. He lit incense every evening and looped voluptuous rings of smoke in front of an altar of cheesy god prints in his kitchen. He washed his hair – and mine – with shikakai. Best of all, in the mornings, while I lazed around in one of his lungis like some feline mystique, he would put the decoction on for filter coffee and then he'd make me dosais.

Perfect round dosais, crisp but still white, ladled out of a stainless steel vessel and spread in concentric circles on a pan that sizzled like rain on summer tarmac or great sex. Dosais the way our grandmothers made them. On every night I spent with him, he ravished my womanliness, and in the mornings, he fed me my childhood.

Some mornings, if I was feeling sulky, I would reject his breakfasts. 'I'm going to Indiresh's,' I'd say. 'He makes *real* maami coffee.' And the Gigolo Maami's lariat of a face would fall. And then I'd take my little stroll of shame over to my friend the Bharatnatyam dancer's apartment, where he would caffeinate me authentically and we would bitch about our boy toys.

'Remind me again why you call him a maami?'

'He makes me dosai in the morning. Can you believe that?'

'Banging can make a girl hungry.'

'Put another vada on that plate, baby, because I am.'

'So what happened today? Burnt dosai? Bitter chutney?'

'He got a mid-coital text from some giggling groupie who spells it L-U-V. And he replied to it, mid-coitally.'

'Ahahahahahaha – this doll of yours is like some sort of satire on the decline of Tamil morals.'

'He is not satire, he is a satyr.'

'One of these days,' said Indiresh darkly, 'that's going to be a problem.'

Then something happened. I met someone else or he took the gigolo thing too far; probably it was both, but either way, months later we bumped into each other at a produce market. We looked at one another across a provocative expanse of fatly phallic purple kathrikai. 'What are you doing here?' I asked.

'Buying groceries. The supermarket near my new house is pathetic. Actually, the whole place is depressing. The watchman is always asleep. The electricity meter is rigged. The water doesn't heat properly. Too many birds – crows shit on my car ten minutes after I wash it. The taps don't close fully. And have you seen the state of the lift?'

'Well, I don't even know where your new house is.'

'Veetuku vaadi, paale pongalaam.'

*Come home, woman, and we can even boil the milk*. What he wanted to sound like he meant, of course, was that we could play at rituals again: tie leaves above the threshold, dab turmeric on new clothes, place milk on the stove and let it rise and run over the pot in a gush of ceremonial good luck.

What he meant, of course, was that I should just come home.

And when I did – *of course* – there was a simmering, and a sugaring. And a grinding and a pressuring and a tasting and a creaming, and finally – a sweetly, hotly overflowing froth.

## THE HIGH PRIESTESS
## NEVER MARRIES

My old flame, the Lucky Bastard, he of the nefarious intentions and the devastating lines, jets back into town on a borrowed Scooty, reeking of pleasant aftershave and profound desperation. He lifts his sunglasses with cinematic somnolence to the top of his curly head, sighs, and says: 'The tides were high and the moon was just rising. If you had come when I called you the other night we could have had epic sex.'

'We've already had epic sex.'

He looks at me. I look at him. He crosses his arms and poses against the bike. He's an archangel but only in profile. He's a cenotaph. Whenever he bit my nose, the diamonds pinned to it disappeared into his mouth.

'Ever heard the story about the chick who

would ride between Pondy and Madras every weekend?' I say as he starts the engine.

'No.'

'So every weekend she could be seen taking the ECR on a Bullet. Up to Madras on Friday, back to Pondy on Sunday. And the highway cops couldn't figure out what the deal was, what it was she was smuggling. They stopped her many times, stripped the bike, never found anything.'

'Maybe she was visiting her boyfriend?'

'Much later, they worked it out – she had been smuggling Bullets.'

It takes a second too long for him to get it, but he laughs. I roll my eyes behind his back. Under my hands, his shoulders are supple and capable of jeopardizing anybody's common sense.

But that isn't going to happen. We are meeting today in the interest of civility and skulduggery, both in the service of parties other than ourselves. His former housemate, the edentulate Swede, needs the vouching of respectable people in order to convince his landlady to extend his lease. He says he doesn't know any respectable people. For the sake of a little booze and a little bribery, I am riding side-saddle in a saree, pretending to be married to this knave, this rapscallion, my former predilection and current accomplice, the Lucky Bastard.

~

I am, as the Lucky Bastard knows only far too well, alarmingly easy to persuade.

At a traffic light, I shout, 'I'm only doing this because you are a family friend and I am a loyal person.'

'Honour-bound as always,' he says, still looking straight ahead. 'Where would the Tamil kalaacharam be without you?'

'Married to you for real, probably.'

'Did you remember to wear the metti?'

'Metti, kolusu, kaapu, pottu, podavai. What more do you want? I draw the line at thaali.' I am a woman who wears altogether too much metal, on the interior as much as on the outside. I jangle like a poltergeist. Kavaca-kundalam ain't got nothing on a girl like a kuthu vilaku.

'Good girl,' he says. 'Such a sweetheart.'

'Always.'

When Erik sees us, his eyes go large. 'You are both looking very, very nice,' he says.

I thank him sincerely. The Lucky Bastard is

too vain to acknowledge compliments; I am vain enough to assume they are actually only meant for me.

I adjust my saree – a chartreuse green with a red print, paired on this occasion with a high-backed Naidu Hall ready-made – a little more than necessary and try to appear demure. The Lucky Bastard cocks an eyebrow, but only after an adorable, inadvertent grin.

The three of us take the stairs to the second floor and ring the doorbell. The woman who answers it is as dour-faced as cautioned, with a permanent wrinkle between her brows that divides her kunguma pottu in almost perfect halves. Her house keys are hooked to her waistband, as is the end of her saree. She gives off the distinct impression that we have interrupted some prayer that could have prevented the apocalypse.

'Maami,' Erik begins, and it's impossible to tell if she has bristled or blushed at the honorific. 'These are my friends, Mr and Mrs Kumar. I used to live with them before I came here.'

'Where?'

'K.K. Nagar,' says the Lucky Bastard.

'Family house?'

'Umm, no, it's a flat. Two bedrooms. We rented one to Erik.'

'Why?'

I keep my eyes firmly focused on the metti on my timid and wifely toes.

'Uh, for some time we thought the rent was high and so…' He's trailing off already. I can sense the panic. All Indian men are secretly terrified of women. It's the state of the nation.

'Your wife works?'

'No…'

'Child?'

'No, no.'

I sneak a look at the boys' faces. The Lucky Bastard's expression is that of an emoticon. Erik wears the archetypal beam of all polite, linguistically-impaired white people in India.

'Why?'

'Sorry?'

'Why no children? How long have you been married?'

'Just two years.'

'Immediately after marriage you rented out room-a?' She looks perplexed. I resist the temptation to tell her that my sex life is hardly in detriment. And neither is the Lucky Bastard's, I'm sure.

'Y-yes. Then Erik moved to your other apartment after one year.'

'And your spare room?'

I interject as quickly as I can. 'For our parents, when they visit. They are in Coimbatore.'

Her face softens for a split second. And then she turns all her attention on me. 'Have you seen a gynaecologist, ma? Maybe you are doing something wrong. You are taking any breast enhancement hormones?'

~

In the end, after a long and painful conversation about everything but his lease, Erik's landlady drops the news that her son is moving back to Chennai from abroad and will live in that apartment upon his return. We trudge down four flights of stairs, dejected, embarrassed and thoroughly pissed.

'Bitch,' snarls the Lucky Bastard. Erik nods gravely.

'She talks,' I say, 'like her tongue is all scratched up from drinking too much pineapple juice to induce a Tamil movie abortion.'

The Lucky Bastard snorts appreciatively. The cockles of my cold black heart warm slightly.

'Well I still owe you guys drinks,' offers Erik. 'And you look too nice to waste on going home.

Unless, umm –' His eyes shift quickly, suggestively.

'No,' we both say at once. I look at the Lucky Bastard and am not sure if I'm relieved or offended.

'We'll do drinks,' I concede. 'No sense wasting this saree, after all.'

And I make a show of asking for Erik's hand to climb into the high seats of his Endeavour, while the Lucky Bastard, smouldering behind his sex-bomb sunglasses, remains perfectly unreadable. Like a sphinx. Like Tamil letters on a billboard when I'm on a bike that's moving too fast.

~

The waiter wears a nametag that says '7 Hills'. 'Elumalai!' I screech in comprehension, and understand, at the same instant the boys do, that this has to be my final drink of the night.

'When are you going back to Coimbatore?' I ask the Lucky Bastard, most needlessly.

'Next week, maybe.'

'Why are you even here?'

'Some work.'

'Did you come all the way here to help Erik?'

'No. I came for other reasons.'

'You break my heart when you're cryptic.'

'You break my heart all the time.'

I am dangerously happy. Something erupts at the next table, a woman shouting at a man, a spilt drink, a shattered glass. Erik snaps.

'Okay guys, it's time to call it a night.'

'Yes yes, watch him now as he forgets he's supposed to pay the bill,' says the Lucky Bastard, in Tamil.

'I don't have any money, do you?'

'Why should we? We did him a favour.'

'I'm sure he'll pay. Don't embarrass him.'

'This son of a whore really embarrassed us today. How quickly you forget.'

'Okay, you guys have to stop speaking a language I don't understand. It's rude. Good night.' Erik swiftly takes out his wallet, removes three crisp thousand-rupee notes, places the edge of an empty martini glass over them, stands up, pushes his chair back in tidily, and walks towards the door.

'What the fuck was that?' exclaims the Lucky Bastard.

'Nordic anger,' I sigh. 'Whatte cool.'

He shakes his head in the direction of the door and watches it for a few moments, as though he expects an indignant return. Then he summons Mr 7 Hills for the cheque, places the cash into the folder and smiles at me almost – almost – sadly. And then something happens.

'So it's just you and me, kannamma.'

It's like someone aimed a rubber band at my heart and didn't miss. I have waited my whole fucking life for someone to call me kannamma.

'I have waited my whole fucking life for someone to call me kannamma,' I say.

He looks at me. I look at him.

'I'll take you home.'

'Just put me in an auto, please.'

'No chance.' And then he takes my hands, both of them, and kisses them.

I like my fights dirty, my vodka neat and my romance anachronistic. He even carries my heels when I decide I can't walk in them, gets a plastic bag for them and hangs it on the handlebar. I rest my head on his back and watch the city as it zips by sideways. And then, of course, it starts to rain.

~

We take shelter under the flyover and share a cigarette.

'You're not coming home with me.' It isn't a question.

'No.'

'You and I could be the culmination of centuries of human longing.'

'Don't tell me about longing.'

A strong gust of wind sends the tops of the trees at the park and the American consulate circling. How beautiful this city, or perhaps any in the world, is to a woman who knows her own bed awaits her even as she lingers, barefoot in the rain at midnight, pretending for just a few minutes that she doesn't know everything she already knows.

A part of me wishes I could still burst into tears at will, overflow with arsonist passion, say all the things I would say if I hadn't already come such a long way, such a long, long way.

And because I have nothing else to say and neither does he, he treats me to one of his signature moves – throwing back his hair, looking pensively into the middle distance, then training that heartbreak of a face right at mine only when he's sure he has me hooked. He has raindrops on his lips.

My cell phone rings. It's someone from far away. 'I'll see you on Gtalk in an hour,' I say. 'I'm just coming home from Zara. So I will be delightful.'

'You always are.' She laughs and hangs up.

The Lucky Bastard is waiting for me to finish what I started. Even Gemini Circle is as empty as a morning after at this hour, and I remember one night when we had hit every petrol bunk between

Adyar and Nungambakkam, looking for one that was still open, kissing like fools all the way down Uthamar Gandhi Salai. Everything closes so quickly, before you know it, before you've even had a chance.

And then he gives up. 'Why are you always so damn cool and mysterious? Like an oracle. Like a high priestess.'

'The high priestess,' I start – and then I have to take a breath because I have said this line so many times but never have I said it this way and I want to do it right, do it the way the Lucky Bastard does it – stylish as cinema, sexy as smoke, unforgettable as trauma.

I look him dead in the eyes. 'The high priestess never marries.'

And then his chest heaves in something I recognize as pain but can no longer empathize with. He pulls me into a hug and before I know it, I feel him sob into my neck.

'I know, baby,' I say, and I hold him tight. 'I know.'

# MENAGERIE

Because he was a man and not a lion, the cuckold wanted the same thing they all wanted, which is to say: a simple thing, a thing he would not name except by its contradictions.

Vixen the Vainglorious did not expect to be outfoxed when she met the cuckold. He was a gentleman. He told bad jokes and gargled before he kissed. He had his briefs ironed and talked about the weather when he was uncomfortable. He was supposed to be the memory of a good man that would protect her, later. He was not supposed to be the cautionary tale.

He was polite in bed. She would never be able to figure out whether he didn't know what to do, or if he didn't want to do it. The first time they kissed, she sat in his lap and took his glasses off and saw him for what he was. Her empathy disarmed her. He had grown old without learning how to let himself be loved.

She treaded delicately in the company of other people's secrets, because she never kept her own.

'He smells like an old man,' she would wail to the Ragfish later. 'The hair on his head smells like coconut oil and the hair on his chest smells like talcum powder. And now these things are mnemonics to me.'

And the Ragfish would roll her lidless eyes. 'Oh, chill pill, honey. There will be other ex-boyfriends.'

~

Because she had no eyelids, Ragfish the Reformed was incapable of flicking her lashes at the elephant in the room. Instead, she stared at it openly and served it slices of sour green mangoes with chilli powder.

Sometimes, she clucked her tongue. 'You lusted after the satyr, you love the cuckold, and now you have to live with yourself.'

Sometimes, she cackled. 'If you ask me, it was the perfect paradigm. Sugar for your sweet tooth and castor oil for your soul.'

And sometimes she would crack her knuckles

and sigh with something that shimmered like mercy but wasn't. 'You were right. You were perfect for each other. Maybe the next time you see Love, you tortured creature, grab it by the horns.'

'That man,' the Vixen rued bitterly, 'wouldn't know perfection if it bit him on the nipple. Which, believe me, it has.'

And then she would close her eyes, because she could.

Ragfish the Reformed had still had her pelvic fins when the Vixen met her. This was before she had reformed, when she still gyrated like a washing machine full of dirty laundry, before she settled down to a life of judgement and insurance.

'For an invertebrate, you have an awful lot of skeletons in your closet,' the Vixen observed once.

'The more you have, the less you care,' retorted the Ragfish. But the Vixen knew, even then, that she was lying.

~

When she first met the satyr, Vixen the Vainglorious thought he was like Rochegrosse's chevalier basking in the meadow of maidens. Beautiful as absolution and so utterly self-absorbed that even the reflection on his armour recorded no visage but his own.

'So, of course, you had to have him.' The Ragfish laughed. 'That's terribly unoriginal.'

'Oh it took a little more contemplation than that.'

'I'm sure ... Spare me the sordid philosophy. And then you met the cuckold.'

'And he was a cuckold long before I met him.' Vixen the Vainglorious paused to light a cigarillo. 'There was a great tradition of cuckolding the cuckold. Apparently all his lady friends did it. The last one among them did it in his own nest, leaving him for one of his own flock.'

'Flock? I never liked that collective.'

'A murmuration of snarling starlings. A pandemonium of perchless parakeets. I know – *a murder*. A murder of crows.'

'Better.'

'I have had six significant love affairs in my twenty-six and a half years,' sighed Vixen the Vainglorious. 'And among them all, the cuckold was the worst. Nobody does damage like the damaged.'

'Six?'

'Six significant.'

'Uh huh,' drawled Ragfish the Reformed,

pursing her fat mouth. 'Well, I don't know how many people I've fucked. Don't remember most, either.'

'Well, if I may misquote Lacan, what does it matter how many lovers you've had if you didn't enjoy sleeping with any of them?'

'Touché.' The Ragfish narrowed her permanent gaze. 'Have you considered how both satyrs and cuckolds are cornuted?'

The Vixen laughed, because she hadn't. 'So am I, in a manner of speaking.'

'You were looking for a lion. It's not your fault you wandered into a glass menagerie.'

~

After he left her, there was no place left to go but to the other one. 'You don't know this, but sometimes I watch you when you sleep,' the satyr whispered into her wet ear, tenderly, and the vainglorious one thought only and immediately of Picasso's minotaur leaning over an oblivious woman in her slumber, his buttocks taut and his eyes closed, balanced on his knees and fists so as to keep his weight off her. Breathing on her dreams.

She was suddenly cold. 'I have to go,' she said. 'I have lost my bearings in this labyrinth.'

Because the satyr would not drive her there, she walked down to the beach to find the Ragfish. They lingered on the shore and watched a weak moon spider its way up a gun-metal sky.

'The horns on his head did not fit the holes in mine,' wept the Vixen.

'There, there,' said the Ragfish, cradling the vanquished Vixen, and as the dark gave way to day and the day gave way to dark, she kept saying it, as though she held a compass that revealed a clear way forward. 'There, there.'

Vixen the Vainglorious stayed still in saltwater for a long time after. Heart like a lighthouse, cutting across the darkness for something equally without safe harbour.

## TAKE THE WEATHER WITH YOU

Before I went to see The Meteorologist for the last time, I took off all my silver. The silent mango-vined anklets, the rondache of a ring from Kashmir, all the bangles except the one that can't be removed. Even my watch, which was probably stainless steel. He had never seen me bare of metal, not even in bed. I had never before guarded against possibility of lightning.

I cannot remember if the day was bright or overcast. Only that when I had first sat across from him in his balcony, the tree it faced had been in flower, and now it no longer was.

But I know I left before nightfall, a net of glories glittering over one shoulder, and that night, when it fell, had been bereft of stars.

I had waited weeks for The Meteorologist to find a place for me in his almanac. It rested on the table between us. In it were all the equinoxes that had passed since he first began to count them; if a record of me existed among them, I would never know. He had something to say to me, but I had hours to spare and days to come that would go unfilled but for the memory of this conversation. I made him take the time he would not give me.

I ate slowly. It bothered him when his dog, in its wisdom, came and laid its head on my lap and lent its warmth to me until he asked it to leave. It bothered him that he could not read my temperature, that nobody called on him or me, that not a single scheduled contingency occurred as it ought to have.

During the first storm of that year, I had seen a man on top of a building adjacent to my home. The roof had no boundary walls, nothing that would protect him in the event of misstep, curiosity, or impulse. He stood very still for a few minutes in the downpour, like it did not occur to him to move. It was unclear whether he had already been standing when the skies broke open over him, or if he had climbed a ladder in the rain to get there. We can forecast nothing. It arrives when it arrives. It disappears when it disappears.

The Meteorologist served mangoes, as we all did in those months of heat and blossom. We were in their final weeks. 'How was the season this year?'

I swallowed a spoonful and remembered the first harvest. 'Not as sweet as expected.'

But while it lasts, we have our fill.

'There are at least seven types of trees known as the umbrella tree,' I said.

I wanted to talk about patterns of engagement and withdrawal, but it's impossible to discuss commerce in the midst of a transaction. You can only watch it as it plays out, and count the coins you are left with later. I wished I had been left with coins – with copper, with something of weight. Instead I felt only as though I carried with me pocketfuls of paper money in a currency turned obsolete overnight, all of it unspent.

He had been speaking but I must not have been listening, because he suddenly raised his voice. 'Like too much atmospheric pressure,' he said, and paused so I had to look him in the face. Beads of sweat had formed on it. I wanted to kiss his hairline where it receded and tell him he was a fool.

I did, but without the kissing.

And then I looked out into the leaves of the tree, softly swaying in the breeze, looked at the light and shadow that was peculiar to his house alone, and said inside myself, *I love you, I love you, I love you.*

'You're a tempest,' he declared. And then, with less cruelty, 'I envy those with turbulence inside them. I am far too sedate.'

He lit another cigarette. 'But you can weather anything.'

What he understood as science I understood with divination. He was as precise as a metronome. I was pure caprice. When I wanted to know if the water was warm, I would wade into it and see. When I wanted to know what the climate was like, I opened a window and leaned out of it. He could sit in his balcony all day and cast measurements, the opera conductor of the troposphere. I knew no such calculations.

Instead, I augured things by what the body told me: if the solar plexus quavered as though having heard thunder, if the bottom of the belly whirred like a vortex of air, if the heart stirred, sensing a pageant of gathering clouds.

*I love you, I love you, I love –*

'You want me to walk you to the door?'

'No.' There was so much wind in my ears.

The tips of my fingers tingled. Something was

spinning, not like a cyclone or a wheel, but like a web, some deeply arachnid matrix. I was barefoot and on the chair before he could stop me.

A foot on the ledge of the balcony, another in the wrought-iron arabesque of a railing.

What happened next was a sort of parachuting. I spread my arms and then I brought it all, all of it, the firmament I raised my eyes to in pain and in praise and by which he marshalled his life, into the cradle of my palms. The labyrinth in my being turned into the gossamer in which I ensnared it all.

'What are you doing?' he shouted behind me.

'Nothing,' I said, and I hauled the sky in with one heartfelt wrench. 'Nothing. Just looking for a silver lining.'

# THE BLACK WIDOW

After the poetry reading, after the hours of rum and cola and courtesy, the black widow stands before the mirror and takes her adornments off one by one. She unpins her hair. She had put it up during the party when it had gotten too hot. She remembers rising from an ottoman and coiling a length of jasmine around a freshly-twisted chignon, the evening swirling about her like a river weaving around a rock. She lifts the flower-strand, already wilting, to her nose and breathes it in. She makes audacious eye contact with her reflection. 'Behold,' she whispers to herself, and watches the shape her painted mouth makes. 'This is it: truth and all its consequence. This is who you have become.' She unravels the sari from around her hips. She unhooks the blouse. She only gets to the earrings before she has to call a friend, and then she's standing there in her bra and petticoat, looking at the kohl running down her own face, trying to remember why she had wanted to go home at all. She feels excoriated, prised open like a mangosteen, bared like the heart of Hanuman. As she talks she denudes her hands of their trinkets, her demeanour of its many masks. She sobs. What does any of this mean anyway, if in the end she has to go home only to herself? She looks at her navel sinking in her soft brown belly, the shape of her collarbones under her skin. 'Do you know the recipe for the Madwoman's Martini?' she sighs into the phone. 'Intoxicant of choice: desire, regret or scent of petrichor. Then: seed from the tree of life. Basil from the garland of Andal. Monsoon, to taste. Simmer the first apportionment. Stir in the rest, singing slowly. Muddle the moon.'

'You and your voodoo,' the friend crows. 'You and your goddamn opparis and operas.'

'Our Lady of Night Madness,' laughs the weeping widow.

'Our Lady of the Torchsong.'

'Our Lady of Beautiful Blasphemy.'

They cachinnate like wind chimes in a cyclone. It is one in the morning. The friend has to go; it's been a long day, and although (she says kindly) the black widow has been its star, it has been demanding on them all. The black widow switches off the phone, and then all the lights in the room. She can no longer see herself. She thinks of her body as a soft space to surrender into, her heart as a cavern with its entrance agape. She makes her way to the balcony with soft steps and adjusts the plastic chair so she can lean back and put her feet up into the arabesques of the grill. All alone on a night like this – quiet as confession and blackwidowblue. Oh what she would give, tonight or any night, for a lover's mouth, for a lullaby, for a moon so low it could snag in the conspiracy of branches. And she sits there in the darkness and watches the silhouettes of trees against a city sky blanched with artificial effulgence, and admires the silver rings on her toes, and thinks of how a good reading can unbraid everything. She blows a smokey cloudkiss to the Venus flytrap in the corner and even the Venus flytrap doesn't bite back.

## SKY CLAD

I dreamt last night of a white lion moving through the sadness of all the rooms in which you loved me. It was still dark when I woke in the faint December chill; just delicate enough that I wandered my own rooms with a light shawl about my shoulders, and when in that hour of stillness I brought a cup of coffee to the balcony I sensed more than saw the colour blue: as though the world beyond my window, with its neem trees and bearded bee-eaters and rusty shield-bearers that rained flowers in mango season, had been tinted in selenium. And I thought of the fixed star, Regulus, which you taught me by name as though I would ever be able to identify it. You had bought me rubies, my birthstone, and when I hooked them into my ears to show you their effect, you let your hand brush my cheek as you reached out to touch them. 'It means the star in the heart of the lion,'

110

you said. Your fingers were cold, too cold for July.

Then you dropped your hand to my collarbone, where your fingertips rested like a pianist's, and with your thumb you parted my mouth. 'Regulus, the star of Raphael, the healer.' Against my teeth, your skin tasted of the sea, but when I closed my eyes, I saw a hue like the evening sky, rose-radiant. And then, a kiss like a tide I surfaced from, not knowing I had gone under at all.

It was not the first time you kissed me, or the last time I kissed you. But there was a first time, and a last time, and between these two sprawled a single galaxy – precise in its dimensions yet vast beyond comprehension, studded with so many supernovas.

You taught me how to measure time, to understand the nuances of even its smallest apportionments. And so it transpires that there is now a different sadness for each part of the day. There are two in particular that I enter without resistance: the saudade of half-light, when the sun softens into a crease in the horizon, and earliest morning. I arise each day as if it might be the day when you will return, and I end it knowing it has been one more without you. Out of the temporality of my pining, I reach into deep time, infinite space.

I turn the sandglass of my body over and

over until it is full again with the honeyed seep of memory. I wait for the sirocco, for the wild, disarrayed compass of your hands.

~

There is more than one way to study the skies, and perhaps you knew them all. I listened to everything you taught me, every word you said, but among all the sciences only one truly held me entranced – and that was our synastry, the magic of what drew us into one another's orbits. You wielded a force I can only call gravity.

Of course I remember the first time you kissed me. It was after the night of the new moon, sun in Aries, jacaranda in bloom.

We had been talking all evening and then through the night, as the party around us thinned and the orchard in which it was held grew first steadily darker, then – somehow both slowly and suddenly – was suffused with a persimmon blush.

We who had been lost in conversation for so long found that the space after a laugh is exactly the size of a kiss. I was smiling when you took the glass from my hand and placed it on the ground, and when you tilted my chin and placed your lips over mine. I wanted you and you knew. Your mouth tasted of wine, elation, luminous things. There was no one else there but the two of us, beneath the aegis of a tree prodigious with color. You dappled small sunlit kisses from my mouth down my throat, took the pendant around my neck between your teeth, unbuttoned my blouse, coaxed it off my shoulders, and cupped your warm palms into my bra.

My breasts came alive in the heat of your hands. You took my nipples into your mouth, the right one with its tiny mole, then the left. I watched you suckle me. You can tell a lot about a man from what he does with his eyes when he suckles a woman's breast: if he closes them, trust him. If he doesn't, don't.

You closed your eyes, and when I saw this I closed mine too. A murmuration of mynas swooped not far from us, and I felt their many-winged wildness in my body, in the electricity in my head, in my earth-bound feet.

'In two weeks the moon comes closer to the earth than it has in years,' you said that night, much later, under a sky wild with stars. You would show it to me. And although I could have seen it by myself, with any lover, from any promontory or window in the world, it was with you that I saw it. It was through you that I learnt that beyond everything within our vision were things we could not even imagine, and our great human fallibility is that we never could, not until or unless we saw them come to life before us, take shape, take flesh.

~

'Though I move only in darkness, I consider sunlight my accomplice,' you said.

'You sound feline.' I had known you a fortnight; and in that time I had taken your body into mine like communion, in a sort of amaranthine possession, imploding each time like a pulsar.

'Too much light can blind you,' you said. I rose from the bed and opened the curtains, saw the thrashing shapes of palm fronds in the wind, the moon low in its hammock a perfect dilation, a chatoyant eye in the sky.

~

Of course I remember the last time I kissed you. You had spun away from me and I sought to hold you, still.

In the veranda of your house of shattered mirrors, you and I sat after dinner, the silence between us darker than collyrium. Years or hours

had passed since that morning in the orchard, ripe
with pleasure and possibility. You lit a cigarette and
I watched its smoke halo you. You did not look at
me at all. In one hand you held your burning stick.
In one hand I held my heart aglow with wounds,
and with the other I reached across the table and
placed it over your fist.

I stood.

I remember that moment, before I leaned down
and placed my lips on yours, when you turned
your face to me and I saw that your eyes were an
unconstellated night.

I kissed you then, slowly and hungrily, and
if you felt any other volition but to respond in
kind, you did not show it. You moved with me,
you moved within me. You circled the tip of
your tongue inside the space in my mouth, and I
enclosed my lips around it and sucked it. I nipped
the softness of your lower lip and drank in your
breath. I kissed you without choreography, a kiss
sad as immortality, wise as original sin.

Full on the mouth, with my hand on your heart.

And then you tried to pull away, and when I
did not let you, you stultified me in the tenderest
of ways. You reached behind my ear and unpinned
my hair. In my surprise, you arranged five tiny
kisses across my closed lips, as though stitching

a line of embroidery. So that later, in the blue-drenched days after your departure, I was left with a sorrow I could not even speak of, that tore me apart if I tried. And then you brought your hands down my sides, found mine and halted their fluster. Your cigarette still charring ash in your grip.

I took a step backwards then, and crushed under my heel the hibiscus that had adorned my head. Long separation unbraids memory: I can no longer tell when I knew that it was over: before I had held my hope between my teeth and surrendered it to yours, or after it, when I saw that flower fallen on the floor. What occurred between the two was simpler: merely eternity.

But I can tell you that there is one other version of this story, and whether I dreamt it or it happened this way, it is also difficult to say.

In that version, you bent and picked up my foot to examine the smear of red on its underside. And you took the trampled blossom in your hand and rubbed its wet petals between your thumb and your forefinger. And with that stain you painted circles around my ankles, bordering my soles like a bride's.

I lifted your hand to my mouth and licked the dye off your fingers. Your palms tasted of salt, the blueprint of your destiny unravelling on the heat of my tongue. I rewrote your fate as I seek now to rewrite my own. When you tried to push aside the straps of my dress, I clutched your wrists and held them at a distance from my body. I watched you, enjoying for a moment the power I had ensnared you in. Your flaring nostrils, the air entering and escaping your mouth rapidly, your broad heaving chest, the tension with which you held back your shoulders. I leaned forward and bit the sharp cliff of your jaw. You reeled. In the same moment that I released my grasp, you had me pinned, the edge of the table pressed into the flesh of my ass, my back arched abruptly, my own wrists held down above my head.

In the distance, I thought I heard thunder, the sky rumbling like a lion's throat.

You brought your face close to mine and blew along its outlines. I closed my eyes and felt your breath trace my features as though in silhouette, disturbing on the eyelid, feather-like on the chin, and gasped when I felt the warmth at my ear. Your moistened tongue entered its whorls, and somewhere in the epicentre of my hips a deeper vortex began to spiral. I cried out, bucked under the weight of your embrace. You released my wrists, ran your hands down my body, found the buttons at the top of my blouse and – did you mean to do this? – in one swift rip my dress had come apart, my breasts under it bare, aching with need.

And you saw the stain on my panties, and you laughed, but I grabbed you by the hair and forced you to look me in the eye. With my other hand, I leaned over and slid the panties off, the scent of dark fresh blood rising between us. I dropped them on the floor with the remains of my dress. I was completely naked now, and you watched in silence as I placed my hand on my clit and kneaded it in light circles, ripples that radiated through my entire being, and then slipped a finger into my cunt. Slowly – one deep dip, one more. To be touched, I felt raw inside; to the touch, I felt volcanic. I removed my finger and brought it to your face, ensanguined, the small turquoise ring you had given me bathed in a stunning burgundy. I placed my nail on the tip of the nipple closest to your mouth, and painted concentric circles upon and around it just as you had decorated my feet.

'Now taste me.'

You lowered your mouth to my breast. I felt the moistness of your saliva mingle with the life and death I had excavated from myself, my broken self, my bloodflowering body. And then you moved to the other nipple, sipped from it gently, and then trailed your tongue down the soft cuesta of my belly.

And then you stopped.

'Lick me,' I insisted.

You hesitated. I saw your eyes in that moment, and something extinguished itself.

I reached behind me on the table and my hand encircled the handle of a knife.

I plunged it without looking, and ran – through the melancholic rooms you had loved me in, up the lightless twisting staircase, until I found myself on the terrace, out of breath, shaking violently. You were only seconds behind me, and I was caught in your arms before I could even turn around.

Your shirt was bloody. We tore it off before we could think about it. I dropped to my knees, unzipped your pants – you threw them over the edge of the building – and you wrestled me to the ground, holding my legs apart with your shins. But I was stronger than you in that moment, and I flipped us over, landing in a perfect collision of anatomies – my open inguina, your magnificent cock.

'The first known maps were of the heavens,' you said, your voice desultory as if intoxicated. We were clad in the sky, and it was heavy with clouds the colour of rajiva lilies. Through a parting in that shadow I spied a delicate rapier of lightning. 'Our history is one of projected spaces.'

'Forget everything if you must,' I said. 'Even the perigee moon. Forget it. But don't forget that there are things beyond our seeing. Beyond these projected spaces are depths you will never comprehend. Run, if you'd rather. But know even a planet of your consequence is tethered by the trajectory of its fated orbit.'

And once again, the knife of you deep in my body, I leaned over and kissed you.

Full on the mouth, with my hand on your heart.

~

Our history is one of projected spaces, our future an uncartographed territory. That night, in the first storm of the season, I could no longer tell what it was that we were deluged in: the wetness of our bodies, the wetness of weeping, or the wetness of a sky that prised itself open as though it empathized with the quasar of my yearning. Our skin, everywhere, was beaded with moisture. With your back against the bricks of the terrace, with my knees on either side of your long beautiful corpse, I fucked you flood-fierce, as though the universe depended on it. Rivulets of water ran down my thighs, mingled with blood. I held the hairs on your chest like reins and rode us into deliverance. And when I came, I unfurled my voice not in victory but in lament.

All this was light years ago. The cosmos of my body, deveined of stars, pulsates with memory.

Come back, my shaman of stars. The universe is merciful; it is ourselves we must forgive. I have waited for you so long, in every different hour of every single day, in this shuddering house, in this forsaken country. I have loved you in the old ways.

And so I wait for you in my balcony, before sunrise. And at nightfall I cuspidate my senses so I can intuit your arrival: prowl of paw, coil of wind.

Love is eternal, I know this. And yet, within the promise of endless time is contained that other possibility – that it is longing that is infinite, forgetting that is impossible, that in such expansive darkness, love itself, that old lodestar, is only a chimera, a trick of light, ephemeral as a full moon.

# NINE POSTCARDS FROM THE
# PONDICHERRY BORDER

*'Sometimes I think of you and wonder if you
really happened...'*
– Aamer Hussein, *Nine Postcards from
Sanlucar de Barrameda*

## 1

Each time I leave here, and leave I must, I number these things among those which I leave behind: waking in the quiet cool before sunlight, coffee on the round red table, the tendril of basil at the centre of the open courtyard, the pepper vines curled around the trees at the porch steps and, at night, that mesmeric canopy of stars.

There are parts of the world that imprint themselves on our souls, and we carry them with us ever after. Then there are places where the soul chooses to stay, riveting down a piece of itself, tethering us so that no matter where we journey beyond that point, we are only orbiting.

So whenever I leave, and leave I must, I number my soul too among the things I miss. I come back here, transfixed, possessed, as if under a spell. I have long conceded that this is witch country. Its hold on me is almost ancestral, as though somewhere in this burnt umber earth lies a cosmic umbilical cord.

I would write to you in secret, in some civilized way, if I had such a way. But you have erased my coordinates from your maps, expunged all record of me, forgotten my name. Yet you own nothing of me, not even that which you took away. So I circle and circle back here, to this house of red bricks with its roof open to the light, this strange southern enclave, and like this, I try to reclaim all I have lost, all I have left behind.

## 2

Of course, you and I both know that this territory I have staked hardly belongs to me. I live elsewhere, in the city, a city I constantly attempt to abandon but cannot, wilting there like a plant that cannot tolerate new soil. In the long months that turn, before I know it, into the longer years, I cry out for something that feels intuitive, indigenous. And then I come here.

When I am away I close my eyes and see the entrance of this house, understanding at last why my grandmother spoke so often of a porch in her final days, as though to set eyes again upon that doorway of a home long departed would be enough. When I first came here, I was heavy with recent death. How was I to know that my grief would only widen and deepen, take spate? The things I carry, the things I cannot leave behind no matter how I try. I haven't had a night without disquietude since.

But I am here now, and sleep comes easy. Or perhaps I don't need sleep at all. It seems that the nights begin when the stars start to spark up, and end long after they evanesce, but the small hours between then and the new day are sating enough. Do you know I can hear you dreaming on some days, in another hemisphere? I raise fat rice and fried bitter gourd to my mouth with my fingers and consume your sleeping diagrams with it, the afternoon around me heavy with the slumber of the distant and the lazy. The dreaming and the dead are with me everywhere I go. But here, more than any place else, they come and sit beside me.

I finish my meal, fix a drink, read a little, and I wait here, threading bracelets from fallen leaves and bougainvillea, for whoever comes first: lost loves, ancestors, or those who wake from naps and amble over, well rested, ready to enliven the evening with their rumours, their vendettas, their perfectly ordinary lives.

3

When I first met the drummer, he came across to me the way he comes across to everyone else – moody, lonely, never sober, never sane. A fixture of the environment, a plain fact, and one so easy to dismiss. But then, there was that night when he was playing the ghatam, with me sitting on the djembe beside him, when he suddenly turned to me and said, 'It's like you. You're so cool – you can take *anything*. Except for a compliment.' This is how we became friends.

One of the dogs comes by, sniffing at my feet. His fur is thick and smelly, full of fleas, and he has eyes the colour of mud after rain. Another unlikely friend. I was weeping one day, when you were here and yet so far, in the thicket just beyond the property, and he had come and sat by me. Not a whine, not a bark, not a single demand. Just sat

by me, silently. And that's when I knew he had
called a truce: I had been afraid of him at first, and
like all animals, he had reacted only to what I put
out. I think over that time now and wonder how
I could have been led that far astray, my intuition
deluded on such a profound level, so that I loved
what I should have feared, and feared that which
could love me.

With the dog, I walk back to the thicket now.
There's nothing much to see there. Sometimes,
grazing cows, their dung steaming and fly-studded
in the heat. Sometimes, a snake. Nothing that will
do me harm unless I invite it to.

### 4

The gardener whose name I don't know chops some
aloe vera straight from the ground for me, his sickle
cleaving the leaves so the sap drips on to my fingers
as I walk back to the house. I put it in my hair to
soften it; I will wash it out later tonight, before the
party. My mother is allergic to aloe vera, but I am
not. I have full lips, and she does not. I was once
the ugly child of an exceptionally lovely woman,
and I carry around the fragile vanity of those who
are never secure in their beauty, never quite believe
what their baby feathers moulted to reveal.

She calls every few days, briefly. I do not ever call her.

I want to say that I don't think you know how lovely you are. But maybe you do. You behave like someone who has never had to ask himself if he deserves what he wants. How simply you plucked me, like a flower for your pocket or your hat. How simply I waltzed into your arms, and not seeing your thorns, took your sap to my lips.

For my hair, I have asked the woman who does the laundry to bring me night-blooming jasmine. I want the scent of it lingering after every greeting kiss there will be this evening. I know that in this village and out in the world there are people who believe that it was I who did the bewitching. Only you and I know it isn't true; like all instinctive creatures I was only reacting to what you posed to me. Still, I don't discourage the notion. After my bath, I will perfume my wrists and loop little bells around my ankles.

5

This house sits between two worlds: the Tamil village and the international commune. It is both and it is neither. It is of no world at all but its own.

In the morning we will have breakfast in

Quillapalayam, the drummer and I. He has a new bike, a big one, but I like his old green one. It's reliable, closer to the ground, quieter. More and more, I am beginning to trust things that move slowly, that stick around. We will order omelettes and coffee in that shop along the main road. I will inevitably be distracted by some trinket or top – you cannot find things this pretty in the city I live in, and yet in this tiny settlement, you can – and we will talk about the party. He may be in a bad mood. I may not be hungry, as I sometimes become after intense nights. We may be silent, but it will never be taken for a slight. He and I are direct people. We have sharp tongues and soft hearts.

If he has an errand to run, we will leave Auroville and head into Pondicherry town, where we will have lunch afterwards. Pork at Rendezvous, perhaps, or seafood at Hotel du Parc, where we can sit on the elevated terrace that trembles each time someone walks across it. We will ride up and down the beach twice – where the water breaks on stone reinforcements put in place after the tsunami of 2004 and a single pier juts out with no purpose – make one stop to buy more wine, and then head back. It will be a Sunday, and this quiet town will be quieter still (except for tourists from the city in which I live, whom you can always tell by their bad driving and drunken antics). Knowing the drummer (and I think I do) he may swing around by the shops where men sitting by the windows gawk at us – a wizened man and a little woman on a bike – and taunt them, waving and yelling, 'Look at all the monkeys!' Knowing him, he may even swing around to do it twice.

6

Basho in the seventeenth century: 'Those who remain behind watch the shadow of a traveller's back disappear.' Do you ever think of the love you walked away from? I myself have learnt to love your absence, your aftermath, everything tinged with a brief and bittersweet beauty, like the world after a storm.

7

By six-thirty, on cue with the sunset, the first guests start arriving. There's a birthday being celebrated tonight, and the reasons why I have been alone all afternoon become apparent; deep vessels of food are brought out, freshly cooked – crispy prawns, basmati rice, a rich mutton curry, cottage cheese in pureed spinach for the vegetarians. Bottle after bottle of liquor arrives, mostly wine, for it's the favourite of the lady of the house, whose birthday it is. Everybody air kisses, because this is a European town, but takes their footwear off, because the earth herself, even here, is Indian.

A joint is lit and passed around. The drummer and I take it only briefly, by tacit concurrence; we have hashish and Kodaikanal mushrooms in the rooms upstairs, so we let the social partakers have their fill. The night grows both cooler and mellower, the laughter increasingly louder, the conversations more disorderly. The lady of the house retires to her bed after a last round of kisses and presents. 'The night is young though I no longer am,' she calls to the party, and, as we are meant to, we take this as permission and raise another toast.

And sure enough, there it is, someone drops your name, and I know it is solely because I am within earshot. I smile politely and change the subject. The only reason anyone else remembers you around here is because of me. Because even when I am far away, I am always here. You do not know how many other ghosts I carry. Neither do they.

## 8

Already the night has gone on too long. Someone stands to receive a glass, someone else reaches out to pour more wine for her. There is a moment of disconnection, the glass falls and shatters. The group is at first startled. Then, there is laughter.

I take the confusion of the moment as an opportunity to leave, quietly withdrawing to the house. I refill my own glass in the kitchen and take it up to the rooftop.

I can see them down below – a man and a woman have started to dance. I wonder how many of these people will sleep here tonight. There are beds enough, and warm bodies, and the ride back through the forest road will be too dark at this time for all but the bravest.

I lie down on my back and look up at the sky, one arm under my head, the other across my belly. This is one of my favourite things to do here. I was doing it when I met you, or at least the first time I noticed you – how strange that I cannot remember being introduced to you. It is as though the memory of you only began from that night we were up here talking for hours – me stretched out like this under the stars, you with your back against the roof's inner border. Your words in the

darkness slipping under my skin at the beginning
of an embroidery I did not even observe until it
had become a tapestry. Until all your needles were
in me, and I was stitched through with that sweet,
sweet sting. You were jet-lagged and I could not
sleep. I liked you. I didn't know then that I could
love you.

*Look at all that loves me back*, I whisper to
myself. I fall asleep like this. Down below, someone
has driven their car into the compound and is
blasting the Gypsy Kings from the speakers. It
does not bother me.

## 9

The bricks under my back grow warm. The
drummer comes up and finds me. 'You left me here
all night?' I am a little hurt.

'Savasana,' he says. 'The corpse posture.
Nothing hurts you when it thinks you are dead.'

'Except vultures.'

'None here, baby.' He cackles a little, and gives
me his arm. We go downstairs.

For breakfast, we eat leftover prawns with idlis.
Then we take the bike and go.

Secrets within secrets. This place itself, this
house, this town, the sensation of having fallen

into a surreal portal, is almost a secret. And even here, there are still more secret sanctuaries. We ride farther into the rural interior.

It happens so perfectly that it's almost as though we had planned it. The first time I had been here, the drummer had taken me for a long ride so I could clear my heart of the weight of you. We were heading to the lake where he went when he needed peace, but we had gotten lost, having taken a detour along one stunning dirt avenue lined on both sides by coconut trees.

Somewhere on this unfamiliar trail, I saw her. She faced away from the road but she was unmistakable from any angle.

We stopped and made our way into the undergrowth. 'This is tantric stuff,' said the drummer with a low whistle. 'Serious shit.'

Kali, painted blue, her many arms full, loomed above us in stone. Goddess of weddings and beheadings. I put my hands on her feet and my head on my hands and wept in a way I cannot put into words.

And this much later, here we are, the drummer and I, heading back to the goddess in that grove with offerings to leave at her feet. We seek her as though we know we will find her, with or without maps, within or without memory. Here along this dirt road, in the heart of a village in a forest on the coast, I see them, my friends – the giant red and black butterfly, the wasps, the whispering trees, the wind, the dancing light. Over and over I return, even when all else has become irretrievable, and over and over, what remains, remains. I hold on tight and think, *this is all there is. Look at all there is to love.*

## ANCESTRESS

Among all the stories of the goddess, there is one that is singular as the story of her heartbreak.

Think of her: the goddess bedecked as a bride, awaiting the one she loves. Sixteen years old, perhaps. Small and shy and thrilled and certain. Her hands can't hold still. She can feel her heart beat even in her hair. Think of the wedding, sabotaged: the betrothed god confused by a cockerel's crow at the wrong hour, turning away, thinking that time had dipped into the malefic phase, not knowing or perhaps only not caring what this would mean, what this single heedless decision would change. Think of the gods who sabotaged her: waiting quietly, watching her slowly unravel, believing that she would be able to withstand it, believing as much in her forgiveness as in the righteousness of their act.

Think of the goddess, her groom nowhere to be seen, the appointed midnight hour slipping past as silent as a thing without anklets: the bewilderment she feels as the facts of what has happened sink in and sink in and sink in again, like a creature caught in an undertow at every chance of surfacing.

Think of them telling her – as though they thought it could console her – that she was made for something else, a rejoinder to a demon's perverse boon that he could only meet his end at the hands of a girl-virgin. How could she slay that demon, how could she protect the universe, and all its condescensions, if she was married? Think of her, a long or a little time after: finally comprehending that by 'virgin' all that was meant was that she must belong to herself, a state of the being not of the body. Think of it, amaroidal on the tongue, that rue: of having knowledge that cannot or could not save.

Think of their sombre faces as they told her: she who midwifed being into being, she who husbands it, could not be anyone's consort. Think, then, of her face.

How little they knew her, her saboteurs; they only knew who she, jilted, would become.

In another story of the goddess, in which her grieving husband dances the universe to its destruction and only the dismembering of her corpse can save it, the part of her that fell on this shore was her spine.

Think of it: her spine.

One by one, she broke all of her bangles. She tore the flowers from her hair. The collyrium that lined her eyes siled, wretched, through the sandal paste on her cheeks.

Shattered of heart, consumed by rage, she took the feast that had been prepared for her wedding and jettisoned it on the shore, turning the colours of the sand variegated as gemstones.

And because her destiny left her no choice, she stepped into it. It was a tide that surged towards her, and she could receive it. Or she could drown.

At the furthermost point of the subcontinent, in Kanyakumari, a bay, a sea and an ocean converge at her feet. Her eyes seek the south. The diamonds in her nose cut through the night's darkness, a long-ago lighthouse. The jewels were a gift from a king cobra, and sometimes their brilliance sirened mariners to tragedies. Who can know the narreme of the cosmos? Why do some of us survive, while others become cautionary tales?

Don't tell me you have never known it – a love that leaves you at sea, sifting for your own words in the waves.

Some of her ornaments, she broke. Some she was bequeathed. Some she bought for herself, the mistress of the universe in the souk of the world. Every time I adorn myself I do it to resemble her, she in whose form I was made.

And she waits, they say. For her consort, for the one who will cherish her, for the one who was thwarted from her. (But why did he turn back, why didn't he stay, and wait for another midnight? And wait, for another midnight.) She waits. She waits with all of us who do. Under skies gravid with the light of long-dead stars. Under immersions that threaten the breath in our bodies. In excelsis. In affliction.

I was born in the holy month of the goddess. I married her on the day I turned thirty, in a tiny temple in the hamlet which my paternal great-grandmother, widowed, left a century ago. This is as far as my father can trace his ancestry: to this handful of earth too recondite to appear on a map, its borders protected by a goddess to whom worship is still offered in the Tamil tongue, in the beating of the udukkai drum, in cascades of rosewater and milk.

That day, I knelt before her in the form of an unchiselled black rock underneath the bilva tree sacred to her beloved deserter. And I reached my arms around her and tied three knots of a yellow thread.

And I was her husband. And I was, first and forever, hers.

I do not know who all my ancestors were, but among them was surely one more woman who slept alone. Who placed her faith in this black stone and laid her body down beside it, trusting. Who called the divine by its name, and it named her back as beloved.

Who was that ancestress, a thousand years ago or only two hundred, who laid claim? She who said – here is the border, and here is its goddess, and beyond this no power shall claim me. Who was she who drew that line?

In the story of my own origin is a moment in Kanyakumari in which my mother, days from conceiving me, looked over an outcropping of rock at that farthest cape and saw her, Maayi Ma. She of the stray dogs that masticated the offerings people brought her, before she gave them back to their bringers, sanctified. She who was said to have wandered, an avadhoota unbonded to the world, for six centuries. The saint turned her face upwards and looked straight into my mother's eyes. My mother had been childless for five years.

How simple the ceremony was. Three knots.

And then, turmeric and vermilion. I dipped a finger in water and pressed the powders to where the space between her eyebrows might be, if she wasn't entirely beyond space itself. An eye of holy dusts.

No matter where I find her or how, the goddess sings to me in red. In hibiscus and menses and tear-stained sclera. In battleground sunsets and iron oxide and freshly-committed lovebites. So the sung and the unspoken both tide within me, so that sometimes I carry her without having to consider her current, without having to know her from myself.

And like this I am her tributary, anchored by her weight, buoyed by her grace. She is my provenance, and from her I emerge: from here to the border, from here to the hearth, from here to the heart of the world.

## CYCLONE CROSSING

It's storming in the near distance when Guru arrives. Still dry, on the roof, we see the lightning rapier over the farthest casuarina grove in our line of vision, and then we see him: his fluorescent orange raincoat coming down the long driveway that leads to our house. At our main gate he climbs off his bike and pushes it open, then carefully fastens the bolt behind him. Our main gate is a relic from the time Shravan's uncle had kept cows, but years later, securing it has become a matter of ritual. The ways we keep out the world we seek to live in. We admire the weather for a few more minutes before we go downstairs to greet him, watching him turn off in the direction of the cowshed, bolt the second gate, and arrive slightly breathless on our front porch.

'There she is,' he points to the sky. 'Gathering her skirts for a good piss.' He and Shravan pat each other's shoulders in what men who aren't brothers call a brotherly embrace. I stand there smiling, at a slight distance, and catalogue what is immediately visible of what has changed of him since we last met: the greater grey in his hair and sideburns, the diamond in one earlobe, and above his dense eyebrows, deeper creases. When he finally puts his arms around me, he leans to rest his chin on my shoulder and breathes deeply, smelling me.

'Honeychild, how are you?'

I look into his eyes and they are clear. He has not been drinking.

Another shattering of lightning and Shravan hurries us into the house. It will be upon us any moment, the rain, but we have been preparing for this for hours. Every window has been latched, there are candles and electric torchlights in every room, and we've seen to it that we have enough mineral water and food for a couple of days at least, so we can avoid having to venture out during the immediate aftermath of fallen trees, flood, animal and other fatalities.

'How did you manage to ride *out* of the storm?' asks Shravan. 'We've been up on the roof watching it build up. The clouds zipped by so fast.'

'She's a real motherfucker,' says Guru enigmatically. His orange raincoat is wet; he gives the impression of truly having emerged right out of the cyclone, but he says nothing further.

Somehow, this makes me smile. 'Guru,' I say, with affection. 'Welcome home.'

'Guhan,' says my husband, with profound politeness. 'Welcome.'

This is how we know him – by two names, as though who he is is bisected by the facts of one life and the accident of another.

'I will get us coffee,' says Shravan, and I look at the clock. Four in the evening. Too early, by far, for anything else. But that's how Guru is – and with him, I was a raging afternoon drinker. Afternoon and all times. Some old node in me aches a little with craving.

Guru sets his backpack down by the sofa and I take his raincoat. 'Where are the girls?' he asks.

'At my mother's,' I say. 'For the weekend and a bit.'

'The cyclone will probably hit Chennai too.'

'Yes, but that's not why.'

Guru has come to spend the cyclone with us because his farm-to-table restaurant, twenty-five kilometres north of us, is failing and he would rather wait for the damage to accrue completely before getting his leaking roof fixed. Also, as he told us when he asked, he just wants 'to shut shop and take the weekend off' – with the two of us.

'I hope you'll be comfortable on the sofa. We have a mattress in the library too, if you'd prefer.'

'Thank you.'

'Sure.'

The windows shake.

'Were you afraid of storms when you were a child?'

'I was never a child.'

Guru. I smile, reach for an appropriate response, give up and shake my head. It's been months since we've met, and now he is here for a day or two at least. He has wandered to the ornamental bookshelf, the one meant for visitors, which contains the volumes an idle browser might be intrigued or impressed by. As if by instinct, he plucks out his own slim hardback with uncontained delight. 'Hey, you've got great taste!'

We do, but his book is there because in a deeply drunken moment on his last visit, he placed it there himself. I demur from raising this point. He has most likely, I am too well aware, completely forgotten.

Shravan has prepared the coffee. He brings it in and serves us. The three of us settle down in my living room and allow the evening to begin.

~

Shravan met Guru – Guruguhan – at a motorcycle repair shop. Guru had dropped his wallet on his way out; Shravan called after him. The older gent (and that day, in his pressed khadi kurta, on the way to a lecture by an infamous deconstructionist, Guru was a gent) admired the younger one's moustache. A compliment like that is more than in passing – it was an opening gambit. And Shravan opened up easily, immediately, and ten minutes of conversation was enough for him to take the older gent's business card and call him two days later for a drink. Six months later, Shravan and I would be introduced, under decidedly less incidental circumstances, in the sweltering heat and noise of his brother's engagement. I was there because a cousin of mine had made me come, bribing me with a white lie; later, after enough street-side lime mint coolers and one chaste kiss under the pink mussaenda tree at the corner of Tiger Varadachari Road had already passed between us, Shravan and I both realized it had been a set-up. It was too late by then to blister. Three years before all of this was when I had met Guru. By the time I met Shravan, I had not seen him in almost two. Shravan, ironically, brought Guru back into my life long after I had turned my back on that chapter of it.

Today, he is full of frustration, and as we drink

our coffee in the cyclone's rather entertaining first act, he cannot say enough to criticize his employees. In particular, he blames the deterioration of his business squarely on his head waiter, who has just resigned – taking, in comical incongruity, the bar manager and the stables-keeper with him.

'Do you have any idea how absurd it is – pouring out pegs I can't drink for other people while chasing after chickens at the same time? And of course, there are no more pony rides for the time being, which basically deprives me of ten per cent of my income, but the kids can still feed them if they like. Saves me the trouble of doing it myself.'

'To be honest, I think that might be good for you,' I say. 'You can't be in this business and just delegate. It takes the pleasure out of it.'

'Making cow dung cakes is bullshit.'

I don't find that particularly original, so Guru doesn't get the laugh he wanted. I continue, 'The secret to not going mad, as an agriculturist, is to keep your hands dirty. The mind then has no room to be anything but clean.'

'I was mad, that's why I started a farm.'

The longer I live out here, the deeper my roots lengthen, the less patience I have for such romantic untruths.

Shravan smirks. 'I would say, Guhaji, that you

shouldn't insult us by calling us mad, but I realize you yourself regard that as a compliment.'

Now I laugh.

'Maybe you need to move away from animals and instant food and focus on the crops,' says Shravan. 'Spirulina is lucrative, and you haven't invested enough in it because it isn't fancy.'

'My customers want fancy.'

'Get new ones, and they'll convince your existing ones. Packaging is everything. I told you – Susha will not eat spinach at home, but she eats it on your pizzas.'

'You two aren't in the service industry at all, so you don't really know what you're talking about.'

'Hey man, just trying to be helpful.'

'Jeez, Guru, and how *do* you do the service industry with that delightful personality of yours?' But I'm laughing – it's safe, I think, the three of us here, old friends already accustomed to the idea of the long night ahead.

'Well I'm finding myself more out of it than in it, as everyone already knows.' He sets his mouth in a firm line. 'And at what point during this evening will I get to drown my sorrows in sugarcane?'

'Ya ya, we're well-stocked,' says Shravan.

'But probably best for after dinner, no?' I add. Then Guru looks me in the eye and glances at my stomach in a way so brazen my jaw nearly drops open. I feel my cheeks redden. I'm not pregnant. How stupid, how benighted, of him to assume it. Over and over, in all the years we've known him as a couple, he has reinforced the point: we are domesticated, we are bourgeois. Just because he didn't remarry or breed, he is not.

Yet here he is, under our roof. Needing.

Already, something that prickles at me beyond mere irritation tells me that opening our home to him this evening was less than wise. Over the years, he has come to our gatherings. He has brought thoughtful presents to our daughters' birthday parties. One or both of us has stopped by his farm en route on a longer journey and broken bread with him. He is someone we know well. Our circle of well-wishers and acquaintances is wide. More than a few of them have thorny histories and battle-worn temperaments, traumata that sent them reeling into frontierlands literal and otherwise. But in one sharp moment of clarity, I see that there is nothing exceptional about having reason to recoil from love, from life. What keeps us alive is the refusal.

Poor man. He has no one else.

A long time ago, pondering the unlikelihood of our shared friendship, I thought it was because all three of us loved argument. That we quarrelled like contenders of equal merit and ethics. But how many times did they happen – pointed remarks, one-upmanship, micro-aggressions that would never be picked up on a Richter scale but chafed the ground we gave him little by little by little? When is he going to tilt the axis? He has lived with his self-loathing so long that it isn't enough for him any more.

A bitter thought – how at different points over the last decade, Shravan and I have said to the other, 'Well, he's *your* friend.' Temporarily disowning him so many times. Conceding hospitalities for the sake of each other. And then, forgetting.

Of course I have been at this juncture before, I rue, perhaps even had this thought before. Typical Guru, I curse in my mind. Two minutes ago, I'd been comfortable, candidly engaged. One flick of his eyes and he's dismantled the entire lull.

Shravan reaches over and runs his knuckles along my forearm. I look up, but he isn't looking at me.

'Henry Miller wrote,' Guru is pontificating, 'that there are only two things you can do on a rainy day, and the whores never wasted time playing cards.'

'Well, we have a fine selection of building blocks,

jigsaw puzzles and dolls in our establishment,' says Shravan. 'Would you prefer those?'

'Are you calling me a whore?' He is delighted.

'If you wish,' says Shravan gracefully. And of course, Guru does.

Guru turns to me. 'You are quiet.'

'It hit just when they predicted, didn't they?' I sip my coffee. '3.45 p.m. IST on the Bay of Bengal. They've gotten so good with this stuff.'

'They had to get good, after the tsunami.'

'They've diverted most of the flights to Bangalore today.'

'Oh, it's really bad,' says Shravan. 'There shouldn't even be lightning, unless it's a proper disaster-level category cyclone.'

'Do you have a generator?'

'We've switched it off. It's safer.'

'And if the lights go out?'

'Afraid of the dark, Guhan?'

'It's the fisherpeople, not the farmers, who really bear the brunt,' I say. 'In terms of loss of lives and overall impact.'

'Rich farmers like you have insurance.'

'Now now, Guhan. Like us, you mean.' Shravan points us all out in a triangle.

'Why do you think I've been waiting to get the roof fixed, man?'

I sigh and start a sentence about neglect and think better of it. I know the truth: he lives off his inheritance. The restaurant, the farm, these are just social currency.

Guru excuses himself to go to the bathroom. I move off the couch and on to the carpet and look at my husband across the coffee table. The wind howls; I imagine for a second a circle of protection being blown around our house, our land. When I'd spoken to my mother just an hour ago, she had asked why we hadn't come to the city too. Suddenly, my reason feels so foolish. I hadn't wanted to drive back when it was all over and see at once what the cyclone had done to my work, to my terrain. Instead, I'd chosen this – to stay at home, and have a guest.

'Poor man,' says Shravan, with a deliberate shrug, his eyes on the corridor to the bathroom. 'He has no one else.'

~

The first thing I made for myself was a mango orchard. The first thing, in my entire life, that I dared to give the world stamped with my name.

The rootstocks of the Mysore Badami arrived in a beautiful wooden box, wrapped as though

they were bijoux of glass. With them came three
nursery trees, four feet tall with coronas of dark
leaves that I held delicately between thumb and
finger and stroked. It was a sensation I would
repeat three and five years later, with a more vivid
intensity, with the births of my children. But that
day, when my first trees came into my life, was the
first time I came close to that feeling.

When I had to ask for the blossoming
eucalyptus to be chopped down, I had known
nothing of agriculture. I thought it was a
heartbreak, but the advice was irrefutable. The
eucalyptus would drain the soil, allow little else
to partake of nourishment. Only by relinquishing
it could I create lushness.

So there, in that newly cleared apportionment
of land I had staked out and claimed, I planted.

I placed the contained trees into the furrowed
earth and buried their roots. Then I moved on
to the rootstocks. And finally, the seeds I had
unhusked and disinfected in the sterility of the
city and carried with me like tender offerings. I
held their curved weight in my palms and almost
kissed each one before I concealed them in the soil.
I was embarrassed by the ceremonial dignity and
emotion with which I worked that day. I thought
Shravan's uncle and his bevy of attendants would

laugh at me, but of course they did not. Eventually, I understood: they already knew.

Two days before my wedding, I stole away and drove down to the farm by myself. It would be almost a year before we moved in finally. Only the foundation of the main building had been laid, but there was a caretaker's quarters and the cowshed, and a plethora of verdure in bloom. There, in that April heat, I ripped the first fruit open with my nails and ate it by myself, standing right there beneath the tree that bore it. I had tears in my eyes.

~

I set the first bottle of Old Monk down and the three of us grin at one another around the coffee table. Somehow we have survived three more hours together: I took a long phone call, Shravan and I went to pray at the hour of an undistinguishable twilight, Guru gave us mercy by losing himself in a book for a while. Then we ate – chicken kebabs and naan – and discussed politics, on which thankfully our expressed opinions (even if not our true sentiments) were uniform. Shravan and I favour the left and fear the right. We cannot imagine any sensible, sane or even merely sensitive person to not do the same. Somewhere deep down, however, I have my suspicions about Guru's leanings. His entitlement, his carefully curated persona, his embarrassment around people who make him aware of either of these things – all these suggest affinity with the seat of power, as it stands in this country today.

Still, the familiar topics – the land acquisition bill, the farmer suicides in Vidarbha and closer still in Andhra Pradesh – came out, and we all used cuss words at the right moments and frowned and sighed and maintained perfect civility. Shravan and I have the privilege of formulating and fostering strong beliefs that go beyond personal specifications. Guru has the privilege of not having to have any, and certainly not having to fight for them even if he did. The establishment always protects its own.

'Our first bottle of the night requires a story,' I announce. 'And I have the perfect one.'

'Is it the Theni one?'

'Shravan, I want to tell it!'

'Okay, okay.' He looks at Guru. 'This story is courtesy of my mother, the scandalized atheist.'

'My mother-in-law, god bless her, told me this story,' I advance, triumphantly smiling.

I pause for effect. 'So. I have been told that there is a village near Theni with a deity who not only drinks but likes to show it off.

'He sits tall at the border of the village, and holds a single clay pot into which offerings of liquor are poured year-round. No one knows where the liquor goes, for there is no trace of it, and no smell. You simply go there, make your petition, pour the liquor and come back with more when your prayer has been answered.'

'Fantastic, more pouring of pegs I can't drink,' says Guru.

I go on. 'There is one particular day in Aadi, I am told, an auspicious day. Crowds gather to pour hundreds of litres of alcohol into this small clay vessel held by the god. And nobody knows where the liquid disappears to, but one thing's for sure – on that one day of the year, his eyes turn red. The statue's eyes turn red!'

We drink to mystery. That's the first round.

The second round is to miracles.

The third is to masturbation.

The fourth – and it is clear by now that we are taking turns to choose – is to motherhood. I have just declared this when Guru takes his metal cigarette holder out and puts it on the table.

'What?' he says, to me in particular. 'Do you really expect me to keep to your non-smoking policy when I can't step out?'

Shravan and I exchange glances. 'We've been keeping to it.'

'Well, neither of you smoke unless someone brings a pack.'

'The girls aren't here and if it will make you happy, Guha…' Shravan concedes.

'That's not the point,' I say. 'We maintain this policy year-round on the basis of several principles. One of which is health. And yours, I'm troubled to note, requires noting.'

Last year, Guru called us from a hospital where he'd driven himself with chest pains. It was, it turned out, 'nothing' – that naïve and terrifying 'nothing' that changes everything.

'Four drinks and not one cigarette? That's inhumane.'

And right then, the electricity goes out.

I thought there would be applause at this moment – we've waited hours for it – but instead there's a sense of deflation. My eyes don't adjust quickly enough to see his expression as he does it, but in one elegant motion Guru holds his lighter to the waiting candle and then to the cigarette between his lips.

'Okay, to motherhood, then?'

'The next one, clearly, is to mankind. And I'll forego my share to mark a symbolic protest.'

I knock back my motherhood round without waiting for the two of them.

'Look at this woman – so sober after having drunk half her weight in rum! I'll never get over it,' Shravan grins.

'She is the calm before the storm.'

'And you, Guru,' I retort, 'are a tropical depression.'

They both laugh, one more agreeably than the other.

Then there it is again – that uncomfortable silence that sleeps with one eye open. For a few minutes, we feign attention to the downpour: the elliptical wind patterns and the rain that at once sounds so close and so far away.

'Fuck, Guha,' says Shravan. 'Just imagine if you were still at home. Noah's Ark it would have been, with all those delicious animals of yours.'

I laugh.

'My god, my lord, what would I do if I didn't have your generosity? Water dribbling through my rafters and money dribbling out of my bank account. And everything going two by two except yours truly, oh so blue.'

'You know,' Shravan says frankly, 'we invited you out of common decency. You don't have to turn it into an act of charity.'

But since when is Guru so easily defused? 'Oh but it is,' he says, and I can see the cogs in his head formulating his next line, something devastating and gauche.

'I'm sure you'll find a way to pay us back,' I interject. 'We do eat, after all. And the girls like the road trip. So I hope you haven't fired your cook yet.'

'I have to sleep,' says Shravan. 'I am so very sorry, but I am so very tired.' He kisses my cheek. 'Good night, Mr Guruguhan. Please don't finish my rum or—'

'Or run away with your wife?'

'Or finish my sentences, rather.' He looks at me and hesitates just enough for me to note it. 'Be careful with the candles.'

'I'll come up soon,' I quickly say.

Shravan takes a torchlight, and Guru and I silently watch its glare bob up the staircase. The child's gate at the top swings open and closes. Next, there will be the sound of a door opening, and if he so chooses, closing.

But Guru does not even wait.

'How do you do it – this yoking you call a marriage?'

'Excuse me?'

'This man, this marionette, with his wholesome upbringing and his inability to form a fist.'

'My husband has been very good to you in spite of everything.'

'He is not your husband. No one could husband you. Do you know what the word means? At best he is your permanent lover.'

I want to open my mouth to say that I do not believe in permanence, but I know exactly what he would say. And he would be right, and I would be lying.

Instead I say, 'I know what the word means. We are farmers.'

'Exceedingly literate ones.'

'Well, yes.'

He drains the last of his drink. 'And there was nothing to spite. Nothing happened in spite of anything else.'

I should not refill his glass, but because I need my hands to stop shaking, I do. I rise, because the second bottle is mostly full and therefore heavy. My bangles unstack on my arm with a tinkling as I decant the rum, add ice, mix it with a finger.

He watches me as I do this, acknowledges the fresh glass I have placed before him with a nod. 'When was the last time you pined for something?'

In the candlelight the tip of his cigarette appears eerie. Shadows conceal his eyes.

I settle back on the stool. 'Why would you ask me that?'

He shrugs. I smile.

I lean forward and tell the truth. 'After you, there was nothing left to pine for.'

I catch a minute, smugly smiling nod. 'What did you do with that void, that ... vacancy?'

'I had children. I planted trees. I grew older.' I laugh. 'How long did you think I could hold such a space?'

'I never knew you were holding it.'

'That's a lie.'

'No, it's true. By the time I began to understand, it was too late – you were already lost to me.'

'I was never lost to you, Guru.'

'You never belonged to me, how could I lose you?'

'No. That's not fair. See, this is what exasperates me about you. Always has. The way you have always pretended as though you never meant anything to anyone.' I reach over, flick a cigarette from the tin. 'The way you would send me birthday cards and not sign them. The way you would ignore me in the theatre and then ask me for a light when you saw me during the intermission. How you made me suffer!' I pause, collect myself. 'That you did not feel the same way that I did, I could live with. I did live with. But for you to deny that you were what you were to me was worse than an insult. It was a humiliation.'

He is quiet. Then he picks up the lighter and holds it in front of me. 'Would you like me to light that?'

'Yes.'

He does. 'You were waiting for me.'

I snort. 'Obviously!'

'I meant you were waiting for me to light your cigarette, that's all.'

'Yeah, yeah, that and everything else.'

'Honeychild...'

'No, Guru. I have let you have your way for a long time. All I ask for is some acknowledgement, some decency.'

'I was doing what was best for you.'

'You were doing only what was best for you, as you always do. It was you who was afraid. It was you who just couldn't – who just *couldn't*.'

'I couldn't.'

'You couldn't. I know.'

'Once you accepted my limitations, it was easier to love me.'

'It was only easier to let you leave.'

'Did I?'

'Didn't you?'

He pauses, as if to consider. Outside, there is the sound of a tumble and a crash – too low to be a tree, more likely to be one of the breeding nests we have attached to some trunks. I wonder if there were eggs, fledglings.

'You're right, of course,' he says at last, when I look away from the direction of the noise and back at him. 'It was you who was impossible to let go of.'

~

Shravan comes down shirtless, throwing a shawl around his torso, his green lungi in need of retying.

'So bloody loud. Who could sleep through this?'

'Do you want some rum?'

'Ille ma, kannamma,' he says. 'I want some coffee.'

I get up instantly. 'Let me make it. Please, sit.'

He accepts my stool. I pick up a torchlight and head to the kitchen. The gas stove flares up in a ring of blue flames before I lower the pot of milk on to it. When I switch off the stove and begin to pour it out, I realize I have, unconsciously, made enough for two.

'And for you?' Shravan asks when I bring a pair of tumblers to the table.

'No … If sleep is possible at all, it shouldn't be discouraged with caffeine, I think.'

'Go to sleep then, your husband and I can keep ourselves entertained.'

'I have no doubt.'

'Are you tired?' Shravan has lifted the smaller of our two divans and brought it by the table; gratefully, I stretch out on it while he keeps the stool. He reaches over and touches my arm lightly. 'This way, you can fall asleep if you feel like it.'

'What about the two of you?' I ask.

'Well, I can't sleep in this ruckus. And Guhan never sleeps, of course.'

'That's right. Never,' says Guru.

'Not true,' I say. 'I have seen him sleep plenty of times.'

Both of them keep drinking without response. Shravan was right – I am tired, tired enough that the etiquette of civil engagement means less and less to me as the night wears on. I am also, I think, perhaps a little drunk.

'It's a pretty name you have for your wife,' says Guru. 'Eyes of the mommy.'

'It means "woman precious as the eye",' I snap. As if he didn't know! 'Why must you demote everything from its proper place?'

'Sorry I'm not as proper as you are, my dear.'

'You should be. Sorry, that is.'

'I *am* sorry.'

'I've always called her kannamma,' says Shravan sweetly.

'Yes, she's always wanted someone who would.'

What Shravan says next surprises the both of us, if not for the question itself then for its absence of malice, because even Guru appears confused for a moment. 'What did you call her?'

'What?'

'What did you call her, before, when…'

Neither Guru nor I respond.

'It couldn't have always been honeychild,' Shravan goes on. 'She would have found it patronizing. Wouldn't you?'

'Yes, I suppose I would have.'

Guru's eyes meet mine, and we both look away quickly. What did he call me? There was no one sobriquet, no one special endearment. Mostly, I think he called me by my given name, a sort of unequivocal summoning.

'I had no secret words for your wife, my friend. That is why she is your wife.'

'Jesus, Guru.' I press my hands to my face. 'Don't be so dramatic.'

'Guhaji, will you finish your coffee, then? I'll have it if you won't.' My husband, the pacifist.

'I'll share some,' I add quickly. When Shravan hands me my half, I mouth the words 'thank you'. These are secret words. A marriage is held together in tacit moments: moments of complicity, knowledge if not consent. He nods. He has deflected Guru without my needing to ask.

'Now you'll stay awake, my love,' he says.

'Ah.'

'Regret,' he smiles. I lean over to kiss his temple. Guru is silent, swaying in the dark. Shravan and I link fingers and I know that we're both hoping he will fall asleep soon.

'Take the divan, G,' I say. 'You need it more than I do.' But, of course, he refuses.

'What do you think it was that fell down?' I ask Shravan. 'It sounded like one of the nests.'

'It could be. But it makes no sense to check now.'

'I just hope there weren't any eggs or chicks.'

'We'll look in the morning. There's nothing to be done now.' He stacks the empty tumblers. 'It's better to tally up the collateral damage when it's all over, rather than when things are in progress. As our friend here is doing with his own property.'

'The worst of it is due in a couple of hours, the actual crossing,' says Guru. 'By late morning you'll be in the clear.'

'Yes but we'll have to see what happens to the trees,' frowns Shravan. 'And the new wing we're building.'

'Who asked you to start building now?'

'It's not so simple. We had to wait till the labourers were available. And there were complications – some dispute between the headman and the carpenter – and we were behind schedule. And all said, nobody expected this sort of cyclone season.'

'I'll never understand why you live this way. Civilization is an hour's drive from here.'

'Shit and chaos are an hour's drive from here,' I snort. 'And getting closer by the year.'

'You spend less and less time in the city these days too, Guha. We've noticed. What do you have to say about that?'

'I'm a free bird. You two have chicklets you have to raise. Children need cities, movement, the fast life. They're not like us.'

'You don't know my kids, or what I want for them,' I say. 'I want them to carry the countryside for the rest of their lives. I want them to be imprinted.'

'They're not cows to brand. You give them this, they will long for that.'

'Doesn't matter. Let them long, let them leave. But they won't forget.'

'Where do you get these ideas from? You were raised in cities, and you loathed them. Your children will do the same in reverse, and run to where you came from.'

'So let them. You don't understand. Nothing can take away the grounding of having grown up close to nature. Nothing can take away from them the fact of having once had sand in their toes every day, planting vegetables they actually ate later, or having watched prawns being raised out of the river in a net. Somewhere, the memory of these things will matter.'

'And the one or two theme parks decorating the neighbourhood.'

I sigh. 'That's not our fault. We petitioned and everything.'

'I think what Guha's trying to say, baby, is that...'

'What I am trying to say is that those theme parks were put up with people like you in mind.'

'Oh bollocks,' I slap the table. 'Those fuckers

don't have a clue what we want. And stop behaving like you do either.'

'Do you know what you want?'

'I always know exactly what I want.'

'Do you always get it?'

'The two are sometimes mutually exclusive.'

Guru throws back his head and laughs, an unusual gesture for him. 'Mutual and exclusive, huh? Now that's something to chew on.'

A terrible crackling of branches silences us all for a moment. 'I wonder what the girls are doing,' says Shravan.

'They'll be asleep, kanna.'

'Maybe not. Your mother might have let them stay up, on account of the thrill. Do you want to call them?'

'No.'

Shravan catches my eye. 'Okay.'

~

Shravan and I decided to buy land before we decided to marry, the second decision a corollary of the first. Two hours to the north is the metropolis where my retired parents live. Shravan's family is from farther away, and sometimes I sense the mountains in him calling.

But on this arable is where we have made our lives, where we are still making our lives, cautiously observing the likes of Guru and his failures and prudently purchasing bonds and mutual funds. Every April, we harvest my mango orchard. May is perfect for the drying work. December is baby-making weather, and both our children are September babies, born under full moons, with the sun in Leo in the sidereal calendar.

Shravan's uncle had helped us with the loan and managed the land before we moved in. It had taken almost two slow years, during which he had established some of the division of the precinct. We sold the cows, but maintained the spirulina and chillies his uncle had introduced, as well as all the trees we could keep that had already been on the premises. This is why we have fresh coconuts, and neem, and tamarind. We kept all the staff he had hired too, for they knew the land in ways that even years later I suspect remain lacunae in my knowledge.

And on the side, other work: the work we trained in, the work which technology allows us to do at this distance. All the successful farmers, those with only small acreage like ours, do this. We keep an eye on our neighbours too, aware that eventually someone will buy out another. We plan to be the ones to make the purchase. Our friends live at short distances, short by the highway's gauge anyway. Even at the earliest stages of excitement, when so many of us began to move out of the city in pursuit of the pastoral life or what we imagined it to be, we all tacitly knew better than to make colleagues of companions.

Every morning, I seatbelt my sleepy kittens into the backseat of our car and watch Shravan steer up the driveway, past two gates, for the commute to school. Right after the sales of a harvest have been tallied and right before the next seeding begins, I sometimes get that single hour after he has left me to my own whims. And as the years pass, I find that mine have become simpler and simpler: a selfish, unshared slice of cheesecake, a Skype call to a friend who sought and found even farther pastures, shopping online. Then Shravan comes back, we fall back into our patterns of work, and at noon I make the drive to bring our children home from school. I will have had lunch made before I leave, or he will have it ready before we return.

We go to the city once or twice a month, for work or for variety. And we travel, together or apart, taking or leaving our children. There is no blueprint for this life. Each new turn is a new season, and no season that came before it can be held in granted expectation or in dismayed comparison.

~

'You told a story about a hedonistic god,' says Guru, sometime after midnight. Outside, the cyclone continues to swirl; the night is malcontent with sound and provocation. 'To balance it, I will tell a story about an ascetic.'

'And just like our hedonistic god,' Shravan says, picking up the two empty bottles and clinking them together with a laugh, 'where has all the rum gone?'

One more glass for me. Liquor is a lullaby; this thought emerges through its gossamer. Guru straightens his back and clears his throat.

'There is a place called the reef of dreams, and it is the place at which things begin and where they are suspended. Denouements belong elsewhere. But on this reef of dreams is where certain beings gain consciousness for the first time, and when they open their eyes they simultaneously see the stars and the sea. They are born on their sides, gazing at the horizon, and so they do not know how to choose one over the other.

'Those not born on the reef can only access it through grief's serrated edges.

'Once there was a god, a good god as far as these stories go, who grew up and left the reef of dreams. He swam through the seas – I can't tell you how many there were, because some were never meant to be named. This was an ordinary rite of passage. One is born into duty, which is only a more utilitarian word for destiny. Our god wore blueberry beads made of his own tears, and the holy ash of his last life across his chest as though he himself was its cinder.

'He was the god of all who claimed him, god of all things for which they held him accountable. A small god, if you will.

'One day, or perhaps one night, somewhere in the long reverie of his travels, he saw her, and the thousand years before her seemed at once like a mere blink of an eye and a time of blindness.

'Who was she – dryad or goddess, mortal or mermaid, sphinx or fox-woman – oh, but how does it matter? In different lights, she was none of them. In certain evocations, she was all, or one.

'He knew: he would love her, always and in all ways.

'But he also knew: his nature was to roam, whereas hers was to remain. He could not take her back to the reef. He could not take her on his voyages. Her magic was a rooted one, and to venture beyond was to imperil it.

'But their magic had already mingled, and she was in him, and he was in her, and they had each ceased to exist without the other.

'And so they walked together, farther and farther, until they arrived at last at the limen between her home and every elsewhere.

'And here she took his hands and looked him in the eyes and said: *I trust you, my love, I trust you.* And holding his hands thus, she stepped across that line.

'But a force for which no words have been invented, because it is among the unspeakable things, held her riveted, on her side of the material realm. Only her hands, still grasping his, had breached that periphery.

'The only way to let him go, the only way to let her go, was to cut off her hands. They would grow back, she told him, her face contorting in anguish. She shuddered against and within that constraint. Each moment in that suspension was a dismemberment of her consciousness. There is nothing worse than to be between worlds. *Cut them*, she screamed. He could do nothing else. He let go long enough to lift his axe. And he severed her hands, and as they fell away from her he could neither close his eyes nor bear to watch.

'And he carried these amputations with him a long, long way – through seas and oceans, but the reef of dreams comes easily to those who grieve, and so he found himself there with an ease that was almost an insult to all that had transpired in the time since he had left. So when he arrived once more in that site of his origin, he fell to his knees and howled.

'And he held her hands within his and wept himself to sleep with his face in their tenderness.

'In the morning, he woke to find that the pillow of her hands had taken root on the reef of dreams and emerged from that charmed landscape as a tree. A network of slender curving limbs, arrayed with thorns and blood-red blossoms that unfurled in grips and floreos. He found himself under this tigerclaw tree, bereft.

'And he died, as even gods do. Or something in him did, as happens to us all. He curled deep within and imploded like a pulsar. But his pining outlived his desire to live. His consciousness dispersed into the wind, a longing that entered all who opened their eyes on a horizon cleaved into the celestial and the oceanic. And then, all whom these beings touched, with intent or in effect. He turned this yearning into the nucleus of his life, and meditated on it. He stilled the flow in his veins and the play of the senses. An ascetic made of stone. On whom a tigerclaw tree still sheds her petal-like tears – incarnadine, alive.'

Guru never has to say when a story has ended. The listener simply knows.

Shravan speaks first. 'Beautiful. It reminds me of those stories of how it is possible to accidentally pray, hidden in a tree and tossing leaves to pass the time. Not knowing that a sivalingam lies below.'

And the storyteller evaporates, and the man we know is in his place. 'How can a society that worships the cock be anything but patriarchal? Don't you think so, honeychild?'

'It's not just the cock,' says Shravan. 'It's sex. The lingam in the yoni ... Uh. You know.'

I hesitate with my thoughts. But I can't help myself. 'I do not think the sivalingam is sexual intercourse, actually.'

'No?' says Guru. And the look on his face reveals his doubt: he knows me too well to accuse me, simply, of prudery.

'You don't think it's a lingam and yoni, love?' Shravan asks me.

'It is a lingam and a yoni,' I say. 'But look properly at the direction of the organs. Look at how the head of the penis comes out of the vagina, not sealing it but breaking it open.'

And suddenly there are goosebumps on my skin. 'The goddess is not being penetrated,' I tell them. 'She is giving birth.'

'To?'

'To the universe,' I continue. 'In the same way, when I see those shrines with only the goddess' head, the puthu ammans, I do not think she has been decapitated. I think she is taking seed in the earth.'

And for the first time all night, both men are completely silent.

I feel at once exhilarated and embarrassed, as though I have shared a childlike observation, with a child's wonderment.

'Interesting,' says Shravan, finally. And I shrug and smile, as if to let the subject go.

'Interesting,' repeats Guru.

Shravan clears his throat. 'And your ascetic then – what did he do? Spend all his eternities pining for his beloved?'

'Now why,' – and in the dim light Guru's face takes on a slyness I know he does not wish to conceal – 'would he need to do that, when she is already his?'

Terracotta tiles have flown off our rooftop, there is no mistaking it, because something comes crashing through a kitchen window and that's exactly what we find. Shravan disappears upstairs to fetch emergency supplies, tarpaulin and adhesive to patch the hole in the glass temporarily so that rainwater and wind-borne debris do not find their way in.

Guru and I linger in the kitchen, wrapped in our shawls. I've grown so weary as the night passed. Every year, there are cyclones. This is by far the worst one we've encountered, and somewhere along the way – when? – that urbanite romanticizing of rain that I never thought could leave me began to abate.

'Does Shravan know about the garden, at Kashyap's house, the night of the turtle walk?'

He has summoned a memory I am astonished I forgot: how he put his knuckles softly at my collarbone behind the carved haveli door and closed the party behind us so compellingly that, the next morning, no one in the household would meet our eyes. There were things I knew about Guru, a long time ago, that will not be true of Shravan for many years yet. We only know people at the ages we know them at, for the years of our own that we know them in.

'Don't be ridiculous! Why would I tell him something like that?'

'Because you don't know how to keep secrets.'

'Yeah, well, I do know how to forget history.'

He doesn't reply.

'And you were history for a long, long time by the time he became my future.' I cross my arms. 'What's with you, Guru? Men don't have expiry dates. Go find a woman who'll do your accounts for you and give your right hand a rest.'

'You ruined the rest.'

'What are you talking about?'

'You and your smart mouth and your stupid ideas and your secret diary.'

'What? It wasn't a real diary. It was a blog. And it wasn't meant to be a secret. I let many people read it.'

'Where is it now?' I don't have to say anything. 'Destroyed, obviously,' he goes on. 'Look what you've done to yourself. What a waste.'

I'm singed. 'I have a good life. What's so terrible about what I have that the alternative could possibly have been better?' My voice – my voice, why is it so loud? 'And you know what the alternative was. That alternative that you tried so fucking hard to protect me from because it was in my motherfucking best interests.'

He starts to leave. I react reflexively, grabbing his arm to stop him.

In the uncertainty of the moment, I am emboldened. 'Tell me the truth,' I say. 'What was it you came for?'

Guru looks at me – he doesn't say a word. His mouth is at once familiar and nothing like I remember.

'I needed to kiss you again,' he says, simply.

And I don't know what surprises me more – the slap I thunder across that excruciatingly persuasive face of his, or the fact that Shravan comes through the doorway behind me and says in a tone so unmoved that it makes my caesarean sutures hurt, 'That's enough now. Guhan, you will sleep in the living room. There is nowhere else for you to go tonight.'

~

Our daughters sleep in our bed with us because we believe that a library is more important than privacy. But soon, there will be a new wing, with separate bedrooms for each of them. The library is theirs too, and like all else we set out to cultivate, it only seems to grow. The library is also where we make love. Tonight, in the cacophony of the rogue winds that pound our windows, we sit on either end of the room – me on the mattress on the floor, Shravan solemn on the desk. The door is locked.

'So. I guess I'll ask the obvious question. You still love him?'

'I'll always—'

'That's not the right answer.'

I sigh and breathe painfully. The truth? The truth is that the lie, with its bizarre and bittersweet consolation, evades me. 'No, you know what, I don't love him. But I want to, I think.' I open my eyes to look into Shravan's, see the sting I knew I would. But he says nothing further. 'Won't you ask me why?'

Shravan grunts. 'Ask you why? Indulge your stupid anarchist sentiments and completely immature need to complicate?'

'That's cruel!'

'You're cruel.'

I stumble for a response.

'No, really, you are. And do you want to know why? Because for the rest of his pathetic life, that man will love you. And he'll turn up on your porch like a mangy dog over and over, needing your shelter, and every single time, you'll relish it.' He holds his hand up to silence my indignation. 'And I haven't even begun to address what all of this, in turn, does to me.'

'This is difficult for me too, you must understand.'

'I don't.' He pauses. 'I liked Guhan. I fell in love with you. I didn't see it in a complicated way, and I believed that it wasn't, intrinsically, because I didn't want it to be. But he – he did. Always did, perhaps. But now, for certain. And now, you—'

'If I had to choose between him and you, I already chose you. A long time ago.'

'Only because he didn't choose you.'

'I'm grateful for that, you know. I'm grateful for what we have, what we've built, what became of me and my life.'

'Then why—'

And I find that I'm crying in that way you cry when you can't ascertain when the tears began. 'Every day, I choose you. Again and again, every single day, I choose you.'

'My darling, it's not even a question I have to ask myself every day.'

'It's different. I do.'

'No. You allowed him to convince you that your life – our life – is devoid of meaning. You decided to allow him to provide his version of that meaning. A thorn in your side to remind you that you are made of flesh.'

And then I stop crying.

'If you want Guru out of our lives, then that's fine. I will do that. We can have that.'

'Yes, perhaps I want that. But there's something I want more, and I don't know yet what that is.'

'How do I work with that?'

'The same way I work with what you give me.'

'But I—'

But the way my husband looks at me mutes me.

'In the morning,' he says, 'I have to go to Chennai to pick up Susha and Pushpa. I would like to have them come back sooner. And I would very much like Guhan to be out of our house by the time I leave. I will leave this measure entirely in your care.'

~

Measure, he said. How do I measure time – how do I measure my life? As a child, I measured it in books. In my twenties, I measured it in clichés. Now, I measure it in trees, I think, or perhaps in the milestones of my children, the way they spill over as fragile as yolks then shin up as agile as snakes. I measure it in newly seeded earth and freshly fallen fruit. I measure it in seasons, like all earthbound creatures, and I acknowledge it in moments.

I had thought that love kept no ledgers – but worse, love keeps appointments.

My husband upstairs in our bed, asleep or trying to sleep. My ex, my bane, downstairs in my living room passed out on my settee. My house missing something at its core: the rumpus of children is not chaos, it is a charm that inverts it. And me restless in the kitchen inside the throat of a cyclone, keeping time, yes – but also, awkwardly, measuring allegiances.

~

I'm already waiting for Guruguhan to wake up by the time he does: anxiously sitting across from him as he sleeps his drunken, guiltless sleep. The clock ticks very loudly. The night has conceded its grasp, as has the cyclone. As I wait, I am cognizant of the effect of the rising light, even through my own sleepless mist.

There are different ways to wake people. My children require touch. My husband requires sound. Guru can be woken through presence

alone. Something in him never sleeps, always stays
vigilant.

He smiles when he opens his eyes, and so I smile
back. It is only a habit.

I hold out his raincoat and backpack with
neither etiquette nor preamble.

'You're going to have to go, now.'

His eyes swivel around the room for a moment,
as though he is orienting himself. As he does this, I
too pay attention to our surroundings, cast myself
in my mind's eye outside my house and see – it isn't
raining at this very moment, but it is still windy,
and dampness and damage persist everywhere. The
ride back will be grim, the highway a necropolis
of fallen trees; and back home, only destruction
will greet him.

So Guru has wandered through our lives and
left us still living in his wake, I think. But this was
something I always knew. That I would outlive
him, whether in lifespan or experience. And that I
would earn my condescension, even if somewhere
in me there would always be a burl of weakness
that would not allow it to turn to contempt.

I have chosen well, I tell myself, and I have
been well chosen.

Then Guru sits up and takes hold of his things,
places them on his lap. In the faded-indigo mistake

of this early morning, he is only a boy. I knew him once, I think.

'Can I speak to Shravan?'

And I forget the boy, even if he sits before me still. 'For what, permission?'

'To say goodbye. To convey my apologies.'

'I'll do that for you.'

'Does he want me to leave?'

'I want you to leave.'

'I am sorry, Arundhati.'

I nod.

'I have tremendous respect for your husband. He is an upstanding man.'

I nod.

'I am sad I did not get to see your little girls.'

I nod.

'Is this the end, then?'

I nod.

And then I straighten my back and ask him, 'How do you measure your life, Guru?'

By his expression, he assumes the question to be a barb. His eyes narrow. So I continue.

'The sum of it, yes, but the smallest quantum too.' Outside, the sound of a pail of water being thrown – who is that, husband or caretaker, who has begun the day's work? 'I've been thinking about this. If I got what I wanted, in the end, like that

Raymond Carver poem. And I did, you know. And I am sorry for you that you didn't. I am sorry that you watched every last thing you loved walk out of your life, taking the path you had paved for it. But I don't think you ever knew what you truly wanted.'

He nods slowly, exhales. 'Is this how you wish for us to part?'

'On a note of honesty, yes.'

'On a note of judgement.'

'Look at yourself.'

He shakes his head, resolutely.

Asshole, I think. I have forgiven myself, somewhere between the look in my beloved's eyes last night and the look in my own in the mirror this morning, for wanting to love him – this man who sits snarling in front of me, this other man – as though fresh growth could soothe some old mutilation. For always having been quick to anger with him, and then amenable to manipulation. For naming him, mistakenly, as a perennial and not a mercenary. For all that, in the absence of reparations, was treated as forgiven.

He snorts quietly. 'You are so fucking sanctimonious.'

Damn right, I think, and I stand up. Here in this house I built, here in this life I salvaged, here I am.

And nowhere in my dominion will I be spoken to
that way. And there is nowhere – listen close, for
this is the great secret that evades them all, all who
submit to the logic of others, and all who entrap
another in their own – there is nowhere that is not
within my dominion.

'Our very best wishes to you, Guruguhan. Take
good care.'

Guru looks at me, a slow confusion spreading
on his face. Shravan comes in through the front
door, his timing as impeccable as ever. He sees the
tableau and instantly gathers it. I see him make
the calculations, and I see myself tallied in them.
In one hand he keeps the door firmly open, in the
other he holds a small axe. It takes him only two
seconds to find the perfect thing to say.

'Guhaji, I trust you're well rested! Your bike is
safely in the cowshed, I just checked on it myself.
And I would shake your hand, but as you can see
I am rather occupied.'

Guru trundles out of our home, carrying his
orange raincoat and the backpack he hasn't even
been allowed the time to put on, faster than an
invective.

Shravan continues to stand at the door, waiting
for him to leave the compound.

'You walked in at the right moment. I think you chased him away.'

'Don't be sore about it. He'd have left anyway.'

I shrug. 'I doubt he'd have let me go without a fight.' I catch his eye. 'That's not what I meant. Not let *me* go. Let the argument end, I mean.'

'Did you get the last word?'

'I don't know, you walked in and stole the show.'

'You *are* sore about it.'

And then he lets the door swing shut and remains standing, suddenly and utterly unreadable. For one frightening moment I am not sure whose voice it is I hear. 'Lovely one, what a strange and remarkable beast you are.'

~

But before Shravan leaves, we take each other's hands and step across the threshold of our home into the ravaged world outside it.

Immediately, we are surrounded by dogs. Wild dogs, we call them, which is not technically true. They roam our land and its neighbouring acres but go uncollared – they belong to themselves, and to the world. When Pushpa was a baby, we tried to have them inside our house, so that she could be raised with animal intelligence. But it didn't work: they unhinged almost immediately into a hungerless sorrow, and would not even set eyes on our child. So we set them into the field and left the door open, and they politely ignored it. A small grey alpha, a gentle bitch with eyes of caramel, a pair of identical collage-coated rowdies, a reserved matriarch with a menacing bark. All of unprovable provenance. They do not even have the indignity of names.

They come to us now and we stroke them, talk to them, check them for wounds.

And then we embark on a survey of our immediate circumstances.

'How did you bear it?' I ask him, sobbing into his chest.

'I didn't see all this,' he says and closes his eyes before speaking again. 'I went straight to the cowshed to check on that bike, because I needed to know if I should call him a taxi.'

We are sitting on a fallen tamarind trunk behind the hollowed shell of the new wing of our house, now a repository of havoc, trying to gather ourselves.

Uprooted trees, branches scattered like leaves. Swathes of pillaged earth that no longer express the crops that had thrived in them. Every flowering

bush beheaded. My beautiful mangoes turned
to firewood. Anything that remains standing is
in palpable anguish, and at one moment I am
uncertain whether the tremble of pain I have felt
is from the orphaned sprigs on the severed limbs,
or from within my own being. We do not find the
nest we feared, only empty ones, but my suspicion
is that Shravan cleared it away earlier, sparing me.
I grip him tightly, knowing the only thanks lies in
never mentioning it.

Never once in all these years of optimism and
lessons and invention have I ever felt, achingly, that
I had torn my heart out and buried it in the earth
and the fruit that it bore was bitter.

I do not think that he will leave me alone in
this, but this is my harvest.

When he goes to start the car, dented slightly
by flying debris but essentially unbroken, I refuse
to go with him. He must have his daughters, he
says. Our house is safe. The worst is over. But
squatting there on that wreckage, I know I cannot
get up even if I tried. I listen to him rumble up the
driveway and away from me. And then, I pray, in
a language more primal than motherhood, more
lonely than atonement. And I put my fingers into
that wet, violated earth and lift it to my mouth,
and I weep and I weep and I weep.

## SALOMÉ

Something is always burning. You will tell me I am hallucinating but I can only know the world through my own senses. The truth reveals itself through veils. I see your hair with its crown of thorns, and I twist my fingers through it and hold you closer. I bite my own lip, and bleed. Your devouring mouth so generous on the caldera of my crotch. I am baptized by your saliva, scorched in skin and nerve and shock. For the rapture it allows me, may the torch of your tongue light your way forward in the coda yet to come. First to the beheading, then to the blood wedding. My beloved, my betrayer, now that you have tasted of fire, how will you ever again walk among a tribe that cannot fathom the scent of smoke? I laugh and I laugh and I laugh, for all the despair I have seen, all the wickedness I have indulged, all the hunger I have ever endured. For the burning ghat of the body, for the abattoir of the heart. And I squeeze my thighs together as I laugh and I hear the crack of bone against bone, a sound like an arquebusade. And then I reach down, the silver coiled around my wrists a cacophony of delight, and pick your gorgeous head up and bring it to my face. Your eyes are still lanterned with surprise when I kiss you. Your lips, luscious with lava, are still warm.

## AFTERNOON SEX

A long time ago, somewhere between the year of personal vendetta and the year of night madness, a fortune-teller looked into my face and said, 'You are both very beautiful and very unlucky. The two are not mutually exclusive.' Then he covered the lines of the palm he had been examining with his other hand and squeezed it as if in apology, for what he had told me perhaps, or perhaps only for having told me nothing I did not already know.

The morning after the first time my husband left me, I woke up with a coin of pain at the centres of each of those palms. They intensified in strikes of lightning that forked down the sides of my wrists. This was before we were married, before he came back, both of which occurred in the year of impossible miracles. All night, I had held the weight of his leaving across a complicated

193

dreamscape, tethering him to me by my very lifeline. My hands, a begging bowl.

I had begged him to come back to me and he had, but contained within that first departure was every betrayal that was to come. I could never unremember it. My husband never betrayed me, in intent or in deed. I cannot say the same for myself.

~

Raghav lives beside the ocean, in a third-floor flat from which you can see it from any eastward window: clear and placid, almost moodless from a particular distance. In the thirteen years that I have known him, he has considered this his only address. He had moved to that flat when he had first come to the city as a student, and he chose not to leave, even when he could have. It was I who moved, from house to house, handed over from parent to hostel to relative to husband. Even when I left Madras I had legal guardians. A poet I knew told me once that men migrate from region to region, but the displacement of women occurs lifelong, in less heroic fragments: from household to household, from keeper to keeper.

It is a small flat, too small for the person he has become, but it contains – as he told me once, parting my lips with his thumb – everything he needs for the duration of his life: water supply, a working kitchen, all his equipment and gadgetry, a mattress, a view of the sea and, on noteworthy occasion, me.

I was still in school when I first met him. He was friends with the brothers in the house across from mine. They were only four years older than me, but at the time it felt like an extraordinary distance. If they had also been children only so long ago, it did not show: they had bridged the interim with marijuana and subtitled films, British Council events, drives to Mahabalipuram, girlfriends. Raghav and I didn't get together until the end of my own first year in college, when he found me standing under an awning at Moore Market one day, watching the rain drip from its eaves, bored and self-conscious and nervous and all of seventeen, my hair in two long braids, shifting a plastic bag of secondhand books from arm to arm.

I had observed him, with no more than a passing curiosity, for years. I was shocked that he knew me at all, let alone by name.

I still lived with my grandparents then, on the ground floor of a cramped house in Parry's Corner. Valmiki Nagar was at the other end of the world. But this is how I first became aware of the city:

because of those long bus rides, the brazenness with which I skipped classes or invented extracurricular events, the exigency with which I rushed home afterwards. One takes for granted the place in which they have spent all their lives. Only a jolt, an uprooting or bereavement, reveals its true nature. For me, exhilarated by my newly electric body, this was how I understood that the city, too, was a sentient creature; by criss-crossing its arteries almost daily, I learnt its heart.

~

These days, it's a different sort of crossing.

I still arrive at odd hours: after noon, most usually, and sometimes I stand in that unkempt kitchen and cook lunch for the second time that day. Raghav is easy to please. For him, food is a matter of sustenance: eggs scrambled with diced onions, tomatoes and aubergines, tossed with whatever sauces he has in the fridge, are enough for him. For Ravi, I cook to enchant and pamper, to comfort and indulge. For Ravi, I cook with love.

I know now that to love someone your whole life isn't a promise, it's a reckoning. I will love my husband my whole life because he will love me all of his, and simplistic math suggests that I will outlive him by at least two decades. I will love Raghav my whole life because I cannot help it: at seventeen, at twenty-three, and as I round the final cusp of my third decade he is still here, where he always has been: shore-facing, tide-aligned, constant, and finally, after everything, without caprice.

After a point, it wearied me to use any other word. It is the only one that doesn't demand an explanation. I love him and I love him. I have Venus in Gemini and stand with each foot in a different river, girdling the chaos of my life with a single, inexorable word.

Two kinds of love then: simplistic and fatalistic.

I used to like to say, about Raghav and me, that our second stab at a relationship was nearly a literal one. I was twenty-three to his twenty-seven; he had made his first film, and we had reunited after one of the many lacunae that cairned our relationship. That was the electric boogaloo, the year of total delirium. It ended in a mutual destruction that would have consumed much more if I hadn't, in a fit of fury and a stroke of luck (how epileptic, the things that drive us to ruin or redemption in heartsick moments), taken a teaching fellowship and fled the city. I came back two years later, strengthened, shrewder, and refused for a long time to meet Raghav except in certain social tableaux in which he had no currency, where I could crush him underfoot like a cigarette while simultaneously asking him to light one.

Raghav and I always knew what the other was thinking. With Ravi, I anticipated his needs, as astute spouses do. With Raghav there was simply no guile. We knew each other too well. We were each other's deepest secrets.

Which is why, that afternoon, as I grated the cheese I had brought back from Auroville over the weekend over his standard egg gallimaufry, my mind wandering to that shocking thing I had done in a rage to the viewfinder of his camera all those years ago, he said: 'So when you left me and disappeared into the mountains or wherever the fuck you were for two years, did you know that every time I thought of you, I saw red? Blood red. Kola veri, baby. Must have been all the lipstick and crayons you left me with.'

I don't remember if it was oil or acrylic but it did what it needed to do. I'd painted the viewfinder. Then he'd taken a fork to one of my canvases – though to be honest it was barely more than that, sketched but unpainted. A *fork*. And then we had thrown plates at one another: to the dish he hurled against a wall I retaliated with a succession of plates aimed right at him. The karmic conversion of this, thinking of that incident in the same kitchen where it had happened, made me chuckle. That was our last major altercation for a while. When he screamed at me to get out of his sight, I took the cue and vanished: within weeks, I had moved to Ooty.

'Those,' I said, thinking of that strange period of retreat and revival, 'were the wilderness years.'

'Wild years, maybe,' he said. 'But wilderness? Choose your words with care. You're the housewife now. It is I, in the end, who turned out to be the hermit.'

I married Ravi two years ago. He was forty-eight, a novelist, a sweet and formal man, my sweetheart, my cherished one.

'Why must you always dichotomize things? I believe in ambiguity.'

'Well, you're a moral relativist.'

'Of course I am. Fucker.' I laughed. 'Don't bite the hand, et cetera.'

He snorted, squeezed my waist with one hand, turned off the tap with the other. His mid-thirties were being kind to him, imbuing in him a deeper, less feverish, lure. He cultivated more facial hair now, and creases had begun to appear, in attractive patterns, on his skin. If he had overwhelmed me as a teenager just by the happenstance of his masculinity, I could appreciate it better now than ever before. There was nothing else like it; no body I had ever encountered, no mind I had ever penetrated, exerted such profound persuasion.

We ate lunch and fucked, as was our practice. When I orgasmed, he pulled out of me, removed the condom, and ejaculated on my belly. 'I want to fuck you when you're pregnant,' he grunted. This was a frequently articulated fantasy. Ravi didn't want to have children, believing himself too old. I wanted whatever he wanted, and had ceased to want that which he did not.

'Well,' I said. 'If ever that happens, I'll let you know.'

'And hope to god it isn't mine.'

'And hope to god it isn't yours.'

We laughed, kissed quickly, with teeth.

～

The aubade is for the morning after; the nocturne, for the evening that precedes the act – though sex is not so much an act as an actualization – but what is the word for this: travelling away from my lover and back into the city before darkness, before doubt and rumour. My thighs coated in something like seawater.

I let myself in and find Ravi reading in the second-floor verandah. I move quietly, so I am already by his chair before he knows I am there. And when he raises his head, I meet his mouth, soft, before he looks into my eyes. It's not yet seven in the evening, and everything outside remains perfectly clear in the last light of day: the mango-feathered parrot that vacillates between the branches of two different trees, the tea-green leaves on one, the thulite flowers on the other. I love this hour. It is the hour between one realm and another. It is when I come home.

~

The day I saw the apparition, I had been driving between Ravi's house and my father's. Twilight, as always, was falling. There had been drumming all day off Tank Bund Road; I had heard it when I left in the morning, and I could still hear it as I headed home. The king is dead, I thought. Who else but a king would have so raucous a funeral; if I passed by the particular street in the slum in which he died, I would have to navigate firecrackers and dense traffic. So I avoided the detours, though in truth it would have made little difference: the city was a catchment of cars, one way or another. I wanted to be in time for dinner, because it was my mother's birthday. My parents made it a point to be in the same house on important occasions. Otherwise, under the pretext of caring for my grandparents, she had essentially moved out. I had been in Ooty at the time it happened. It hadn't bothered me at all. When I came back, I had simply set myself up under my father's roof. He asked few questions and I made few demands. He was kind, uncomplaining, unsuspecting and rarely overbearing. My mother, like a bullfight, was best enjoyed from reasonable distances.

When I finally managed to cross the signal after the Chetpet bridge and turn on to the road parallel to the Cooum river, it was a quarter past eight. I was intensely frustrated: to the self-reliance that had come from learning how to drive, I far preferred the insouciance of taking autorickshaws. Not for the first time did I miss the thousands of rides I had spent listening to music, lost in my own thoughts, able to notice everything and yet pay attention to nothing at all. Madras cannot be experienced within a car: one must traverse it unshielded, buffeted by its winds and smells.

To my right was the river in darkness – a scattering of lights visible on the farther bank, a clutch of huts on this one. I was taken in first by the two men collecting laundry off the lines, vast blankets of varied colours which they threw over their shoulders in seamless movements. There was a small fire, by which an old woman was weaving bamboo or some other pliable wood. And then I saw it. Tangled in the trees right above them, her beautiful hair like banyan stranglers, her eyes dramatic and almost lamenting. She looked right at me, blinked twice, and turned her sad face slowly as if to watch me as I accelerated, unnerved yet suddenly in perfect control.

I drove the rest of the way biting down on my lower lip, refusing to think.

Paro, my most intuitive friend, called that night. The birthday dinner was over. 'Antara,' she said, the moment I picked up. 'Antara, what happened?'

That was the night that I learnt about the curative powers of rock salt. I poured a palmful into bathwater and scooped it over my body and head over and over, humming as I did so. I slept well. And when Paro came to visit me three days later as I lay in bed, healing, she knelt beside me and said, 'I was going to ask you quietly, a little later. But this happened so quickly.'

'You knew?'

'Pregnant women see these things.' She kept smoothing my hair away from my forehead. I was woozy with shock and pain. 'Did you know?'

'No. I had no idea.'

I had been blindsided by pain that morning, intense and somewhere deep in my body, and then a terrible sense that that something had flowered, but in blood. I had had the sense to make a few phone calls; it was Murthy's girlfriend who had taken me to the gynae. At the hospital, I was given the medication and told to go home and rest as I bled the vestiges out, and see what came up later. My father, bless him, had noticed nothing amiss when he came home.

'It was still very early. You wouldn't even have known if you hadn't been in such pain. Sometimes these things pass like very heavy periods. Were you late?'

'Yes, but I hadn't really been thinking about it. I guess this saves me an abortion, anyway. They were horrible enough at the hospital as it was.'

Paro drew back her hand, as though slighted. 'Why do you say that?'

'Because…'

'You can't think like that. Why would you think like that?' She put her arms around me and held me as she must hold her own children in their illnesses. I remember that I fell asleep that way, a sleep full of dreams. None of them were important: they were an exquisite corpse of unrelated parts, and yet they filled me with dread. None of them predicted my choices over the coming year, the year of my undoing, and neither did they predict what others would choose for or against me, then or later.

These days, Paro still has her gifts for nurturing and insight, though they are encumbered somewhat by her growing comfort in her life as wife and mother. Paro has been married since she was eighteen. She has a certain innate understanding of relationships that only people who have not suffered the disorientation of too many of them can have.

'What's the difference between a happy woman and a trapeze artist?' She offers kind, but pointed, riddles in times of particular chagrin.

She is a happy woman, and because of this she bears no judgement. I know it is I, in my ardour and avarice, who sometimes looks askance at her life, with its ordinary domesticity, its unchallenging contentment.

'Do you remember when you taught me about cleansing with salt?'

'Of course, I do.'

'Is it okay if the salt is on the rim of a margarita glass?'

She laughs, and covers her teeth with one hand. We meet for lunch every fortnight. She needs a respite from her kids and her husband; I simply need her. It is good to have a woman friend who knows. There are only three people from whom no secrets have been kept. Madhu and Murthy, the twins who had been my neighbours when I first met Raghav, are the other two. They know us the way we know each other. They are implicated in ways that go beyond loyalty and trespass into the arena of blood ties.

On the subjects of loyalty and trespass, I have experienced much, and known very little.

'Sometimes I bathe with salt after having been with Raghav. I guess it's a sort of guilt.'

'Hmm.'

She takes a long sip and smiles. 'You know, don't you ever wonder if maybe Ravi is fully aware? I think it's just an arrangement that works for everybody concerned.'

'I couldn't respect a man who thinks that sort of cuckolding is okay,' I say. And then I'm surprised, because I hadn't realized that I believe this, and I'm surprised again in the next instant to find that I do.

'You are a wicked woman!' She laughs again. 'Have your cake and eat them both – is that how it goes?'

'But it's not really about sex, you know.'

'I know.'

'I've explained this.'

'I know.' She smacks the table lightly. 'So don't use words like guilt, na? I thought you had it all covered.'

'I don't. Relationships are about constant negotiation and re-negotiation.'

'But all the negotiations are in your own mind.'

'Yes, but…' Paro never exasperates me. I need these conversations. If I didn't have them, I truly would be running circles in my own head. She challenges me. I take a deep breath. 'The problem is, Paro, that there is no known paradigm. Men have always been granted multiplicity. But when women do it, it becomes duplicity.'

'That's actually true.' She frowns thoughtfully.

'Yes,' I say, and I'm more relieved than I thought I would be. 'Yes.'

Later, as we hug goodbye in the parking lot, I ask her, 'You'll never condemn me, will you, Paro?'

'I never have, darling.'

'Thank you.' I kiss her cheek.

'No problem. Just keep your eyes open and

your heart … you know.' She winks, squeezes my hand, walks away.

~

The year of impossible miracles was preceded by the year of my undoing. It seems, in a certain neutral perspective, to have been a very brief sliver of time in which I came undone. Although undone doesn't quite describe what happened. In Tamil, there is a word: arundhu. It means a sort of unravelling. Like a string of beads coming loose. This is the word that comes closest to the visceral memory I have of that time and the watermark it left in my life. An unspooling.

Ravi came back and strung me back together. He sequenced my disorder. But first he left, and before he left, I did all the things that concluded in his leaving. Raghav was not one of them.

~

Ravi works every day, for hours at a stretch. The first year we were together he made some sweet-tempered attempts at accommodating my presence into his schedule. He would try and work at our common table, putting his feet up and scribbling away on a notepad while I sat across, reading or thinking. If it didn't work for him, he didn't complain, but I found it tedious and oppressive. 'The problem is I'm always working,' I finally explained. 'I mean, when I'm alone with my thoughts. It's work. I'm sure it is for you also, when you're alone with your thoughts.'

'Okay.' He smiled sagaciously, kissed me generously, and from then on has stayed in his quarters, generating a steady five hundred words a day, while I wander the house, wander the Internet, wander the city. I watch films, meet friends, listen to music, indulge my melancholies. I pick up my brushes on average once, at most twice, a month. When I do, by most accounts, I disappear for days at a time. I draw all morning and then eat lunch alone – Indian-Chinese food ordered in, straight from the tub with a plastic fork, contemplating my easel. And then I paint. But just after sunset, I clean up. I rinse my tools, draw the curtains, lock my room – an old habit from the days of homes with no privacy. I shower lightly once, and then I start to cook. And when the meal is ready I shower again. I shave my legs, wear a dress, gems. I rim my eyes and, if it has dried, braid my hair with jasmine. Dinner, on days on which Ravi and I have both worked all day, is special.

One of the little things I love the most about my husband is that he hums before he wants to kiss me, especially if this occurs at a less than obvious moment. I think it is a sort of expression of shyness, of which he is probably totally unaware. I learnt to read it very early in our relationship, and it is an observation I keep to myself, a little delight. If he believes that I want to kiss him as much as he wants to kiss me, he is right. There is never a wrong moment.

The pleasure of preparing a meal for the man one adores. For Ravi, I de-shell every prawn individually, because he talks while he eats, and chokes on them. I slide a nail into the crease at each underbelly, devein it of the black intestinal cord. I toss fennel and mustard seed into oil, add curry leaves, boil the prawns, then introduce them into a simmer pungent with onions. I turn bitter gourd sweet by caramelizing it in jaggery. I steep the rice with coconut milk, a signature ingredient. I peel and slice an avocado, smother it in honey from a mangosteen orchard, and leave the confection in the freezer. For Ravi, anything.

I cover each dish with a lid, slip into the bedroom, blow him a kiss when he looks up from his book. I bathe and perfume and paint myself. When I come out, he is waiting by the dresser with the strand of rose quartz he had given me for my most recent birthday. This is our ritual: I watch us in the mirror, a woman whose eyes become like light on water as her beloved loops a rosary of his devotion around her neck.

He chooses the ornament, and to it I match the outfit. Tonight, a gray sheath dress with a pink ribbon at the waist. I admire myself for a moment or two before going out to join him.

In our house, we go barefoot. I wear the metti, the silver matrimonial toe-rings, because I love their weight, and I love the way they clink against tiles when I walk. I tinkle my way towards him as he stands by the kitchen counter, slip my arms around him from the back, sniff a kiss into his spine. He hands me my plate, already laden with the food I have cooked. 'Thank you, my love,' I say, and tiptoe to kiss his cheek.

'Thank *you*,' he says. 'Look at what you've made for us.'

'My pleasure,' I say. By which I mean, 'My privilege.'

~

This is not the trajectory I had been on; this was not the life I should have had. I am grateful for it in ways that I am incapable of expressing adequately.

'When do we get to see what you've worked on today?' he asks between bites. I like watching him eat. My husband eats passionately, as though he has hungered a long time and then finally been allowed to partake. On his plate, curd and curry mingle with the dark sauce of the jaggery, and he scoops and licks the pulp from his fingers with relish.

'I'm estimating three days. It's acrylic, so it won't take long. It should be done by tomorrow, if I work at the pace I did today, but I'm leaving a little legroom.'

'What is it?'

'The Vasundhara commission.'

'Ah,' he says, in a way that means, 'Remind me.'

'Something for their guest bedroom, not too large. A 30x30, to go above a corner table. Her brief said the female form, a suggestion of rain clouds, red lotuses.'

'Sounds like calendar art.'

'Exactly why she thought of me.' I grin. I am an indolent painter with a better reputation than I deserve. I love my art and will fight for it as all artists do their own. But I like, even foster, the slight incredulity I have towards my career. It keeps me grateful. Ravi smiles. He is the most unassuming genius I know. It is because of his humility that the concept even occurred to me as a trait to cultivate.

'I can't wait to see it,' he says, and I know he means it. We run this household together as equals: his books and journalism bring in a bigger income than my paintings do, but I make up the difference by managing daily administration. Apropos of neither, we share a deep mutual respect for the other's work. This is what I value: that we are a household that creates, not one that destroys.

'You are in charge of the mundane and the miraculous, both,' he had said to me once, as we made up over one of the domestic disputes that chequered the initial stages of our living together. That was the year of the dishcloth, I joked to someone once. But really it was the year of deliverance.

The mundane and the miraculous, he said. But I had married Ravi because he *was* the miracle. I was a trainwreck; he was the railroad switch.

He had gifted me normalcy, routine, security. He had lifted me out of the abysmal chaos of my life and allowed me to occupy his.

I ladle more bitter gourd for myself, refill his tumbler with chilled water, and contemplate the notion for a moment. Marriage as occupation. Occupation: the principal vocation of one's life. The source of one's livelihood. The state of being occupied.

To occupy: to take over, to fill the whole of, to possess, to seize, to invade.

He believes I am not ambitious enough, but I suspect these things are easy to say for a man in his place. When he was twenty-nine, the same age I am now, Ravi's first book won an important international prize. Publishing in India wasn't then what it has now become. The book changed his circumstances and freed him to write whatever he chose. It allowed him to lend his voice to causes that moved him. It eased his life. I am not sure what an equivalent meteoric rise for a woman painter today may be. Perhaps there has never been such a thing.

Besides, for a long time I have harboured the misgiving that major success would discomfit me. I am happy to paint for myself, for my small circle of patrons, and where my name or my work has resonance beyond my association to my famous husband, I am happy to go.

I am fulfilled in profound measure by my

smaller persona, my relative obscurity, my secret lives. The sum of them is more than enough.

~

He begins with my fingertips. He kisses each of them in turn, and then finally, slowly, slips his mouth over one, so it is grazed on one length by his teeth and along the other by the wet warmth of his tongue. His back is to the kitchen sink – it is he who was cornered, for I slid my arms around him as he finished washing the plates, I pressed my body against his and inhaled the scent of him, lifting his shirt and slipping my hands beneath it, reaching for the dark dials of his nipples so that by the time he put the last plate away his breathing had shallowed and I did not need to lower my touch to his pyjamas to know that he was hard, inveigled, incandesced with desire. He took my hands away from his body, clasped them in his, and turned around and took them to his lips.

And when he finally moves his mouth away from my fingers, I am a creature of pure nerve: ichorous, turned to nectar.

I cannot wait long enough to get to the bedroom, so I loosen his buttons standing right there in the kitchen, bury my face into the white hairs of his chest, and he lifts me by the hips and pins me to a wall. I lift my legs and hook them around him, and as we kiss his crotch grinds into mine, a perfect, delicious pressure. I could come like this, but I am glad I don't, because in the next instant he has dropped me back down softly, only to roll up the hem of my dress and slip off my panties. I am still up against the wall, one leg thrown over his shoulder, and he takes his tongue to me lightly once, twice, and then slithers it, precise and rapid, against my clit for one intense and overpowering moment until I moan and then he looks up at me, he looks up at me and he says, 'Can I take you to bed now?' as though it were even a question.

And we are there before I even know it, our clothes reflexively discarded, our bodies ravenous. I lick the length of his thigh, I kiss a trail of teeth down his vertebrae, he takes the wet of my cunt to my breasts and anoints my nipples before he sucks them. We are quicksilver, magma, an avalanche of skin and hair, heat and ardour. Finally I cry out as I lower myself on to his cock and undulate around it, surge and swell, pitch and pivot. When he comes he is silent, capitulated, except to say over and over, 'Antarayami, Antarayami, Antarayami,' baptizing me with my own name, reaffirming my presence, my power, my very existence.

~

Raghav and I go up to smoke on the roof, and the sea swells gently beneath a cloudless sky, a morose aquamarine. Very little separates this block of flats from the ocean. As the crow flies, and this is literal, for Madras is a city of crows, this is all that lies between: an empty lot, a quiet street, a stone wall, two small houses, a single garish temple and then the beach. I have come here in so many moods, over so many years. I have wept here, alone. I have stood under a full moon and kissed him here, during a time when I had wanted no one else, when I belonged to him as I have never belonged to anyone since.

When we go back downstairs, we find Madhu in the living room, rolling a joint. Although Raghav laughs, exclaims 'Machan!' and meets the other man in a half-hug half-handshake, something in his body language when we enter the apartment indicates the same alarm I feel to find Madhu here, so arbitrarily, just minutes after our tryst.

'Had some work at Kalakshetra Colony, so just dropped by, man.' Madhu's eyes rove over to me. 'You all didn't lock the door.'

'Just went to the terrace, da. Anyway, want anything? Juice?'

'I'll just split this and be on my way.' He licks and seals the joint, and hands it to me decorously. 'Ladies first, madam.'

'Okay.' I light it, take a single quick puff, and immediately pass it to Raghav.

'How are you, Anukutty?'

'I'm good. You?'

'Good ya. Work is picking up nicely. A lot more coming in suddenly. Still painting?'

'Yeah, of course.'

'Husband still writing?'

Raghav coughs, gives the joint to Madhu, and interjects, 'Husband's always writing. Clever bugger he is.'

'Oh yeah?'

'Well,' I say. 'That he is.'

'Clever or a bugger?' Madhu chortles at his own joke.

'Fuckers, you think you know everything.' I'm annoyed but not really threatened. The twins have always been like this. They gave Raghav hell when he started going out with me, but whenever we fought, they jumped to my defence like they were my own brothers.

'Your husband is an old man. In ten years you'll be picking out his bones from the burning ground.'

I don't balk. 'For my necklace of skulls, right?'

They both laugh.

'I am heading back your way. If you want, I can drop you off at your place.'

I consider it, but before I can decide, Raghav says, 'Yeah, you didn't drive today, did you? May as well.'

'Okay,' I say.

Something about Madhu bothers me today, and I cannot place my finger on what it could be. I leave the men to their chat and wander to one of the rooms, where I sit at the window and flip through a magazine. A bottle of nail varnish lies under the divan. I pick it up idly and read its name. *Sabotage*. It is a shade I would identify as cerise. Raghav sees other women, mostly foreigners who visit for a few weeks or months – travellers, eager girls studying music or dance for a semester, working artists of varied inclinations. He was never, not even when I was a girl and a student myself, faithful to me: a fact I only accepted well after any semblance of a conventional relationship had been proved impossible.

I don't have any delusions about the ethicality of any of this, but there's no chance to contemplate them anyway, because Raghav appears in the doorway before I can begin the thought. 'So, he wants to get going.'

'Okay, I'm ready to leave.'

'Want to take that with you?' He means the nail varnish. 'She's not coming back.'

'No, thanks,' I say. 'Not my shade.'

~

Small talk all the way back into town, but as we cross the Teynampet traffic junction I figure it out. 'How's … Sindhu? That's her name, right?' Girlfriend of a few months, whom I had met once at a wedding – my hand on Ravi's forearm and my eyes evading Raghav.

'Yeah, that's her name.'

I should have been able to read his tone but it doesn't strike me. 'Yeah, Sindhu, how is she?'

'Fine and dandy, I'm sure.'

'Oh.'

'You didn't hear?'

Shit. 'Hear what?'

'She left me, man. She fucking cheated and then she decided to leave.'

'God, I'm sorry about that.' I am.

'Yeah, well. What can you do right?'

I don't really say anything. He switches to Tamil, and his voice takes on a huskier timbre. 'I was friends with that dog. He was Murthy's brother-in-law's friend. He was almost family, man. She fucked him in my house. You know who told me? That maami who lives on the same floor. Do you know how she told me? She asked if my wife had a brother. How could I tell her, she was neither my wife, and nor was he her brother? I really lost my pride.'

I truly do not know how to respond. Madhu is in more pain than I have seen him in in years. He keeps going.

'So I confronted her, and she didn't even lie to me. She could just have lied to me. I would have believed anything she told me. I gave her so much, how easily I would have believed...' His voice breaks. 'Instead, she said all of it was true and she had just been thinking of how to tell me, because she was going to leave me. Leave me to be with him.'

'I'm so sorry.'

'And then she did.'

'When did this happen?'

'About ten days back,' he says in a way that means exactly ten days back.

'Do you want to stop and have a coffee, a drink? Or you can just come home if you like. Just sit and talk to me for a little bit.'

'Thanks, da.' He wipes his eyes. 'That would be good.'

Then he reaches over, smiling sadly, and grazes his knuckles against my cheekbone. 'What will you tell your husband?'

'Won't have to tell him anything,' I say, and smile firmly. 'Just as long as you don't.'

~

But Ravi appears to not be at home; the watchman says he left half an hour ago. I make Madhu the milky tea he asks for and sit with him at our common table outside the kitchen. He talks to me for what might be a long time. People in suffering pack their sentences with words and silences so loaded that each of them must be weighed like precious cargo, passing through customs.

'I can't believe you didn't know any of this,' he says finally. 'Raghav didn't tell you?'

'You could have told me. I don't actually see Raghav very often.'

'I mean, Antara, Anu … Why do you live like this? Why can't you just pick one?'

'Pick one?'

'I mean, in a burning house, who would you save?'

I am incredulous. 'So now my life is a hypothetical premise to you? What is this, the Proust questionnaire?'

Madhu doesn't answer, but takes a handkerchief out to wipe his face with. He looks older than I ever recall having noticed. 'I'm sorry, Madhu,' I say. 'I know you're in pain, but that doesn't mean you can negate someone else's situation. Or disqualify it because it isn't like yours. We are all equally wretched.'

'You are not just someone. I am telling you this because you are someone I love. And you are hurting people.'

'No, I'm not. I'm not hurting Raghav because this is how he wants it. I'm not hurting Ravi because this is how we function. This is our marriage. This is what we have built, together and apart. I will fight tooth and nail to protect it. That *is* my moral compass.'

'Then why did you go crazy when you lost that baby?'

This has me blindsided. 'I went crazy because I lost a baby! What can't you understand about that?'

'You were crazy because you felt guilty.'

'What?'

'I always thought that was it – like you thought you had been punished because you wouldn't even have been able to tell whose it was.'

'No,' I say, and the blood in my head pounds. 'The baby was Ravi's.'

'Maybe you're confused.'

'There's no confusion. There was no one but him at the time. No one but him.' I push my chair back and stand up, steady my hands on the table. 'Get out of my house.'

'Why are you being such a bitch, Antara?'

I am weeping openly now, overcome with anger and a complicated grief. 'Get out of my house!'

'Look, I didn't mean to upset you. Jesus. I just thought we were having a conversation.'

He grabs his bag, his car keys, and keeps looking at me in a strange, almost bewildered, way. He reaches the door and turns around. 'I'm sorry if I upset you. Take care. I am sorry.'

And then he is gone, and I stand there shaking like a leaf in a storm, like a sheet on a tin roof with all the rivets coming loose.

~

Ravi finds me an hour later, eating condensed milk sandwiches. He knows this is a code. He knows this is from my childhood: it is what I do when something defeats me so utterly that I cannot be consoled by talking about it, it cannot even be absorbed by alcohol. He comes and sits beside me and rubs my back. When I indicate that it has been enough, he goes to the next room, where our gramophone is. And he puts on a record in Portuguese, something profoundly mournful. This is also a code. This is what my husband does when he is held to ransom by a grief so precise it will not survive translation.

~

I have said before that it was my hands that were a begging bowl during the year that he and I were separated. But my heart, too, was a bowl. Or more accurately, there was a weight in my chest each night as I tried to fall asleep, and that weight evinced the precise sensation of a terracotta bowl filled with beads, or seeds. The contents of this vessel stirred at every provocation, susurrus. This is an elaborate metaphor, I know. But this is how I experienced the most fragile moments of that very long year during which I was suspended between volition and vulnerability like an electric wire between poles.

Shortly after the miscarriage, I went to church for the first and only time in my life. The truth is, when I boarded the 29C outside the El Dorado building I wasn't entirely sure what my motivations were. The bus went almost as far as Valmiki Nagar. I had not seen Raghav in a year or two, but the memory of him was still coiled somewhere deep in my body, a potential, possibly gravitational, energy. I was still shocked by how that body had betrayed me, first by allowing itself to be embedded, and then by rescinding its decision. I was implacably restless and had begun to take long walks. I think I took that bus because it was a mnemonic for a simpler time, a time of elation and self-possession.

It was only once I was on the bus that it occurred to me that this was not the route that belonged to that time. Still, I had a seat and earphones, and I watched the city through the metal railings. Gemini Circle, the Chola Sheraton flyover; this was before the hoardings were taken down, and all over the city, advertisements and aspirations stood higher than most buildings. At the Kapaleeshwarar temple stop, I half considered getting down, if only because the city's older areas offered a sort of altered consciousness of geography and personal history. But something held me back, either heat or indecision. The still water of the temple tank was a compelling green, either peacock or phthalocyanine. I pondered it until it was out of sight. The Ramakrishna Mission, the Adyar bridge, and finally, the turn towards the Besant Nagar depot. This was when I disembarked. I had no desire to go to the bus depot. I intended to walk to the beach.

But I didn't get that far. Instead, I found myself buying a candle outside the church. Elliot's Beach was bookended by two loci of the holy feminine: a Catholic church on one end, and the former home of the mysterious, marvellous and recently deceased choreographer Chandralekha on the other. I bought a single orange candle, lit its wick with the light of another, melted the wax at its end against the heat of another, and placed it into one of the holders at the altar of flames in front of the shrine of Mary.

And then I joined a small queue by the side of the building, and made my way to the image of the Virgin of Vailankanni. I put my hands up to the glass for a long moment, and breathed.

Outside the church, I wanted to catch an auto back but didn't get one for a reasonable price.

I walked down the street, past vendors selling religious images, keychains, paraphernalia. I crossed at the supermarket, kept walking.

I cannot be sure what caught my eye first: the assemblage of necklaces spread on a piece of tarpaulin, or the little girl walking across the sky.

She was doing more than simply walking – she was *dancing*, one foot in front of the other on a cord slim as a reed, swaying from side to side rapidly so the tightrope moved in tandem; her head erect, her lower body pendulous. In her hands she held a balancing stick. Two bright golden champa flowers stuck out from behind each ear like horns. I stood, transfixed, five feet below her, as she crossed the tightrope swiftly, steadily, and broke into an exuberant grin when she arrived at one end. She crowed down to the man selling the necklaces in Vagriboli. When he raised his head to cheer back, I saw that something in his nose and jaw was just like the girl's. He was her father or uncle. He had a scar from the edge of his smile to the top of his cheekbone, like a comet. The Narikuravars are the most beautiful people in south India. Honey-eyed, dark-skinned, with faces elegant as the foxes for which they are named, they are our gypsies: vagrant, subterranean, maligned.

The woman beside him was less ebullient, but

when she raised her eyes to me I saw they were mischievous, complex. 'Anything for you?' she asked me in Tamil. 'See this.' She held up a chain of deep yellow stones. 'Or this.' In her other hand, a clutch of cowrie shells. She looked like a sort of minor goddess, her palms extended and filled with bijoux, sitting within the nimbus of her sequin-spangled crimson skirt.

'No,' I said. 'I'm just looking.'

The child back-flipped from her post and landed on the asphalt. If her bare feet were scorched by the road, she didn't show it, bowing and curtsying repeatedly and with relish. The woman was watching me, and though she did not ask again if I would purchase anything or reward the little acrobat's performance, I intuited the meaning of her gaze. I took out ten rupees and held them out for the girl but she had already begun to clamber up the frame of her apparatus, this time with two steel rings in her hands.

When I turned back to her, the woman took the money from me, smiled, and pressed two roses the colour of burning embers into my palm. 'These,' she said, 'are for you.'

~

The experience meant nothing or it meant everything. The magical is everywhere, as is the surreal, as is the grotesque. These are things I had always inherently believed, but something about that incident stayed with me. Over the next year, I turned its motifs over in my mind and let them take on elongated values. I contemplated balance, suspension, gravity, ornamentation. I painted like a demon. My father did not condone liquor-drinking for women but I took to bringing quarter bottles of state-manufactured vodka or rum into the house, which I hid and mixed with juice. I was doing very well for myself, artistically, for the first time since my spell in Ooty, which in some ways was not dissimilar but had lacked what I had come to accrue in the intervening years: a few group exhibits, at least two good magazine profiles, a small but advantageous bit of international travel, and of course, my sudden and glamorous role as the significant other of a noted and charming man.

There is a chronology to how things happened, of course, but memory is always corrupted, disarranged. This is the progression as I can best reconstruct it: I had a miscarriage just a few months after meeting Ravi, neither of us fully understood the weight of it, I threw myself into my work with manic fervour, I studied tarot, I experimented with reiki, I drank as though I would never die, yet lived as though I feared it constantly. I read portents in everything, until the universe turned into a tragedy of tangled live wires. I got back in touch with all my exes: Raghav of course, the other teacher in Ooty, the other painter in Ooty, the beautiful actress, the two boys I had dated between my first and second relationships with Raghav. I took a train to Kanyakumari and bawled into the sea. I moved out of my father's house and into an apartment, and then into a hostel when I could no longer afford it. I fought with Ravi and I fought with Ravi and I fought with Ravi until finally he said to me, 'Antara, nobody can fix you but yourself. Do it and come and find me. I'll still be here when you do.'

I didn't even understand what that meant, but I know that when he left for Berlin a few days later to deliver a lecture and give some readings, I became intensely paranoid that he would cheat on me. And when my grandfather died in his sleep that week I called him sixteen times at 3.00 a.m., German time, and when I did not hear back from him until after the funeral, I refused to listen to reason, refused to believe that his phone had malfunctioned, and when he cut his trip short to come home to me I threw every fragile object within my reach at him until there was nothing left that could possibly be broken.

'If you cross my threshold again, I will kill myself,' I said.

He stood in the frame of the door with my father behind him. They looked in that moment remarkably similar: two ageing men, hunched in disappointment and sorrow, their expressions perfect replicas.

'Listen to me when I tell you what I will do,' I said. And he did. He left me because I asked him to. In the year it took me to find my way back to myself, I thought the scaffolding of my life had collapsed, but in my suffering, city and society folded me quietly back under their custody. Custody – another intricate word. I moved back in with my father, and my mother and grandmother followed suit. I took a hiatus from my work, cancelled all my commissions. I gave my time to children in a slum near Pallavan Salai, teaching them drawing, crafts, self-expression. I invented and performed ceremonies of release: once, a kite knotted with handwritten messages; another time, an offering of flowers set into the sea with a song. For my lost baby, my never-born and only child. I wish I could say I painted my way back into the world, that my art lit a passage for me out of my turmoil, that I walked out of a place of incineration carrying my own burning heart before me like a torch. But this is what transpired: at some point I stopped lying to my parents, stopped living in conflict with my ecosystem. I eased cautiously into a more rational way of life, and when somewhere deep down I despaired that I could no longer recognize myself, I called the man who held up the only mirror in which I could bear to see myself completely: mad, miraculous, mundane. And I begged him to take me back.

~

Ravi and I met at a dinner party at the home of mutual friends: Paro and her father, a retired high court judge with a fair degree of clout in important circles. The party was held in the honour of a guest of his from England, and Ravi was acquainted with both of these gentlemen. I was invited mostly on account of being an old friend of his daughter's, but was introduced proudly as one of India's most exciting emerging artists, a conceit I quite enjoyed at the time. I drank wine, exchanged business cards, but slipped away as often as I could to hang out with Paro's kids as they watched TV in a bedroom. That was how I met Ravi. He had come into that room to use the bathroom. Afterwards, he lingered a moment, looking at me in a manner I have never ceased to find irresistible, and when I said hi, he perched himself on the arm of a settee and stayed.

We got married in a forest sanctuary on a morning after it had rained all night, in a grove flush with day lilies, presided by asoka trees, in which butterflies abounded and once again, with perfect eloquence, the world was lush with omen. This was the secret ceremony; a traditional one had already been held in Madras, at the insistence of my parents, who strangely protested far less than I imagined. The guests danced barefoot in the mud and drank white coconut rum from Goa. How many names for the colour of the earth in Tamil Nadu: red ochre, burnt umber, areca, sienna. Afterwards, when the rain started again and we retreated indoors, Ravi held my feet and kissed them as we sat on the porch – the stain of deep orange on my soles, the silver rings around my toes, the sepia of my skin itself.

If my entire life could be reduced to a single image of my own choosing, then that memory would be it. Self-Portrait as Cherished Consort. Nothing can revoke the fact that he had chosen me. If I can keep the amulet of that memory safe for the rest of my life, it in turn will chaperone me through reversal and grief and transformation of all kinds. And the years and the years and the years.

~

I don't expect Ravi to come out of his office while I make his lunch, but he does. I am sitting in the verandah reading the newspaper, waiting for the potatoes to boil, when his door creaks and he steps out. He stretches and yawns like some stylish animal and groans, 'Just wanted some fresh aiiirrrr!' When he raises his arms above his head, his short kurta lifts so I can see the bottom of his belly, softly rounded and lovable. He stalks to the kitchen and I can hear him rooting around in the drawers. He emerges with a spoon and a small tub of butter pecan ice-cream. 'Dessert before lunch,' he says, apologetic. I smile and let him feed me a spoonful. He stays standing beside me and lights a cigarette. It's one of his restless days. Sometimes he does this: seething for days like a cloud gathering moisture, erupting finally in a torrent of inspired brilliance.

He finishes his cigarette and starts to whistle as

he walks away, then pauses. He retraces his steps back to the table and rummages through the books stacked on it. I wait until I hear him humming, and then I tilt my face to look at him, his kind eyes, his sweet, giving mouth.

'Thank you, my love,' I say when it's over, and I tweak his nose, press a kiss on his stomach through his shirt. He caresses the top of my head, kisses me again lightly.

'Going out today?' he asks before he closes his door. And I say, 'Yes, I am.'

～

Which is sadder – to approach a denouement knowing it, or to realize only later that the last time was the last? This is the thought that breezes into my mind as I cut across the city on this sultry afternoon, an old Ilayaraja melody in my ears. It occurs to me at the traffic light on Rajiv Gandhi Salai, a share-auto full of green bananas on my left, a bus teeming with passengers on my right. I blow it away like dandelion spores when the signal changes.

Raghav has just returned from a shoot in southern France. He will have brought back Chablis and Swiss chocolates, or something of equal extravagance. Neither was specifically promised when he texted to let me know that he was back, but these things have become a matter of custom. Just as when we were kids, before any of us learnt how to cook, we ate economically or went hungry, fought over petty bills, ordered cheap take-away or poured hot water over cups of dehydrated noodles and called it plenty. We never considered that there was another way to live, yet here we are: light years between everything we were and everything we have become.

How much and how little changes. I have taken an autorickshaw because I am heavy with memory today. I am wearing a nostalgia piece: a silk scarf we had bought from a Kashmiri merchant in Spencer's Plaza when I was nineteen, an indulgence so heady at the time that even the day of its purchase is unforgettable. I stroke its hem and the intensity of the sentiments it evokes takes my breath away. Here we are in a drive-in movie theatre again, here we are trying mushrooms for the first time in somebody's farmhouse, here we are – fools and lovers, found and lost.

But more than that, more than anything, there is one intangible image that has travelled with me across the distance of a decade … Perhaps this is a composite memory, perhaps it happened over and over, perhaps it never happened at all, but its imprint is vivid beyond contradiction. On his mattress on the floor by the window, Raghav lies on his back, cupping my breasts in his palms as I sit on him. And when for a moment I arch my back and open my eyes, the bright yellow curtain at the window flaps slightly and I catch sight of it, blueness sparkling in the afternoon light. I reach out, hold the end of the curtain up, and gasp, wavering between the pleasure of our bodies and the pleasure of the sight of the sea. It only lasts a second, for he slips out of me, complains and draws me back with a jolt of his hips, but it doesn't matter. In that one moment I have seen it all, I have surfaced: boundless, uncontainable, a feral thing, a force majeure.

## SANDALWOOD MOON

For hours we followed the river shaking in coins of sun until it led at last to a place of stillness. The night swept its wing low over the southern heartland and let the sun slip from its beak. We settled down on the stairs of the old seraglio and looked across at the dovecote, a terracotta lamp on its every sill, and did not question the origin of its splendour. It appeared, simply, to have been lit from within.

And because we were hours from any coast, and because the moon exists only where it is sought to be seen, it would not emerge from the sea that night, an orange smoulder waning to smudged ivory. Instead, midway between the earth and the nearest star, a rondure of sandalwood: a colour I could slough off as balsamic for my skin.

There is a mystery to how war enters a person, and how it can be coaxed to exit without wounds.

There is no mystery to the trajectory of the heart, its arrivals and departures. Amidst the shadows of senescent buildings, flickering lamps, the wind an ineloquent thrashing amongst the coconut fronds, you said, 'How grand the world is. And yet' – you kissed one of my small hands, calyxed within yours – 'how easily encompassed.' I did not respond then. But I knew that after the storm, by the light of day, I would take you to a pond caparisoned by blossoms and try to show you how elongated sadness becomes as delicate as a lily stem and as strong. I would watch you from a farther shore. And if I could not teach you how to love, I would teach myself how to live alone.

This is the weight of love: just because you can touch water doesn't mean that the oceans are yours. This is the weight of grief: buoyant beyond disbelief. I have learnt how to look for both before they come into view: diaphanous, a low-rising ring, light midwifed by light.

# THE HULUPPU-TREE

We were happy in the huluppu-tree, my lion-headed eagle and I. We were friends with the uncharmable snake that helixed in its roots, and we looked after the Anzu babies together. I was the handmaiden of Inanna, the Queen of Heaven, the Lady of Largest Heart. That was then, before the sacred marriage and the holy crap. That was there, in the sacred grove, where Inanna planted the tree of life and I was its keeper. This is neither then nor there, but I am, and I always will be, Lilitu of the Black Moon. I exist wherever you cannot see me.

We were happy in the huluppu-tree, and then one day She thundered into the grove and said we had to go.

'No,' I said, and turned over and pretended to go back to sleep.

'I need your tree to make my trousseau,' She

241

shouted. 'A bed and throne of the trunk, a dowry of the branches.'

With this, I fell heart-first out of the huluppu-tree. 'You're getting *married*?' I screeched.

'Why, yes,' She said. 'To Dumuzi, who will plough me, my uncultivated lands.'

I cocked my eyebrow.

'Why do you have to marry?'

She didn't answer, so I went on. 'Does this mean the end of the rites, does this mean the end of my going into the fields for you and finding them – those eager striplings, those silver foxes?'

Inanna cast Her eyes to the left in a split second of misgiving. She knew I saw it. I always knew everything. She always knew I knew. She told me She adored the young ones, those butter-fed calves, with their muscles like forbidden fruit and their appetites like clockwork. She told me She loved the sight of her black pubic hairs rubbing against Her bullish older lovers' white ones, found this an extraordinary and erotic thing. All this and more She told me, my mistress who – even if She didn't *really* know – really should have known better. But now She was silent, her forehead wrinkled, her expression as brutally beautiful as lapis lazuli.

'Let me stay, Inanna, for I cherish you.'

'You can cherish me from any of the eight directions.'

'Let me remind you of the origin stories, let me soothe your anxieties with all the cantos in your praise.'

'I am only anxious that you leave me be.'

'Then let me write your vows for you, because there is no one who knows better than I of your heart's true desire.'

'You are not a very good writer,' She scoffed.

I was hurt. 'Perhaps not,' I said, and camouflaged myself behind a flabellum of leaves. 'But I do have an arse poetica.'

The next day we woke to a convulsion of chopping noises. We peered over the maze of branches and saw our beloved serpent lying prostrate at the base of the huluppu-tree. She was weeping. 'He smote me,' she cried, through eyes she could not open. 'He smote me – I'm smitten!'

'I thought nothing could enchant her,' rumbled the Anzu, flapping his wings so hard that around us a hurricane of fury started to grow.

'Love is not a spell,' I said. 'Love should not be a weapon.'

A terrible upheaval followed. I felt the huluppu-tree's roots grip desperately at the earth, felt it in my own belly like a twinge of bloodlust or maternal instinct. We swerved. All the Anzus spread their wings instantly, even the babies who hadn't grown their manes yet. They perched on thin air and roared down at Inanna and Her axeman, Gilgamesh the hero with his storm-swept curls. I lifted myself from my nest and glared. She glared right back. And then, when Gilgamesh turned his attention with a bellow to the final and irreconcilable swing, She mouthed the words, with those eyes full of fear and last night's slutty smudged kohl, 'I'm sorry.'

It was then that I turned away, turned tail and talon and every last cinder left of me, taking my snake with me, and my birds, and my curses and my courage and my wisdom and my exquisite and envied damnation. We fled into the mountains. We never left the wilderness.

After my huluppu-tree was destroyed, I made a garden by scattering each kernel of unrequited longing and irrevocable loss I had experienced. One heartache turned into a hot-blooded hibiscus. One cruel twist of fate curved into a caveat of magnolias. One unspeakable trauma clichéd into a cereus cactus, with moon-kissed white petals. One broken promise took wing as a bird of paradise, permanently bent and profoundly beautiful. This is how you live, with the knowledge of all you could not keep. You take all the love you intended for only one thing and you spread it out, wherever it can give succour (having so much, you need not take more). You let it thrive. And you live. I tell you – you'll live.

## MANGO WOOD DRUM

If you were mine I'd give you a mango wood drum and make you forget all your exes, especially the ones who liked your hairy belly too. I'd live each day as if it belongs to a tearaway baby Murugan calendar. I'd try to be quiet when we make love during power cuts. I'd always be as pretty as a pepper vine and I'd teach you the word 'uxorious'. If you were mine, it would be easy for you, and simple for me. Simple like tender coconut ice cream. Simple like a lyric that couldn't have turned out any other way. There would be fat, happy babies and kalamkari kisses (if you want to know what those are, there's only one way to find out). There would be a swing in the balcony and fifty-two honeymoons a year and nothing to regret in the night rain. Who but you could console me? Who but you would ever know how?

## SOMETHING LIKE GRACE

Saltwater is not the sea but it comes close. I stir it with my fingers and watch the granules swirl in the little stainless steel bowl and think of how all my life I have stepped into the ocean in order not to drown. And how on days when the summer has kissed his skin even before I have, I can taste the sea on his body. And, always, in his mouth after he has tasted mine.

He comes into the kitchen as I slip roulettes of sliced bitter gourd into the bowl and asks what I am doing. 'The salt cures it of bitterness,' I say. I turn to accept the drink he has poured us – rum in Coke with ice and lemon – and say, 'This is a secret recipe.' But this is not true: like all things about me, the moment you encounter it all its elements are laid bare.

A special recipe, then. Something I make on a day when he has visited me on a whim, a day which contains a jacaranda in bloom. I walked down the street and met him at the corner so we could admire it together. I stood next to him and squeezed his hand and bit my lip and said, 'Kiss me continentally.' And he did, and the bones of my face, my beloved grandmother's cheekbones, lit rouge from the heat of his breath.

He settles his weight on the counter and opens his notebook. He likes to watch me cook: before we had kissed for the first time, he had made fun of how long I took to cut vegetables but then he'd said, in a voice that sounded almost wounded in its wanting, how nice it was to look at. So this, in the span of weeks, has become ceremony: slow jazz, him by the window that overlooks the street of bangle vendors, and me moving between the kitchen and the verandah, my hands full and damp.

I punch out the seeded white flesh of each piece of bitter gourd with my thumbnail, and throw the excess away. Then I drain the bowl, using my fingers to dam the slices as I hold it over the basin. I set it down, turn to look at him, and smile. I love his five o'clock shadow, I love his fierce imagination. He adjusts his glasses and reads aloud – '*What is sweeter than honey? What is stronger than a lion?*'

'I'll show you,' I say. 'Step out of the kitchen.'

~

My grandfather brought bitter gourd back from Batticaloa yesterday, and today that is what I will make lunch with. He brought it back in his suitcase, through a day and a half of transit – the interminable highway to the capital, the night of abbreviated sleep, the long drive to take the short flight. I ask him to describe buying it, and when he says, 'From a woman selling it by the side of the road in Vandaramulai,' the landscape comes back to me. The miles of intractable longing and the burden of unfeasible knowledge. A bridge that cannot be uncrossed. A lagoon that spills towards the sea like a confession. The memory of my grandparents' country (I will never have one of my own, and by that I mean: I will never have just one, and maybe I will never have even one) is weighted like a saree on a washing line: it will never, not even if dried to chalk, drift away.

When my grandmother died, she left me her thaali. In my life, I was meant to have one nuptial chain.

And by that I mean, maybe only one, or maybe – oh…

The gourds he bought are softer, the skin a waxy yellow, a variant called meluthu-pavakkai. Wax-pavakkai. I hold their texture in my hands and my grandmother's love helixes to life within me, a cherished cerith turning over in the waves.

I gasp with wonder when I cut the second gourd open. Its seeds have ripened, plump and slick, to a beautiful ruby red. Like pomegranate arils. When I cook for my grandfather, I cook from the heart of all that we have lost. I cook from a locked place, in the language of lullabies whose words and tunes I do not remember that I have not forgotten. The nature of all things that we lose is that they can never, not truly, be bigger than all that we have loved.

~

When she says she has enjoyed an aversion to it from childhood, and that nothing but her mother's exasperation could have led to this longing, I laugh and repeat a proverb – *the chick never dies from the hen stepping on it*. She rolls her shining eyes and pushes her shoulders back with a groan, the fact of her own motherhood as irrevocable now as history. She smoothes her strained kurta over her belly and exclaims, 'It's even called pavakkai! The sin-fruit.'

'My pavakkai is as sweet as redemption,' I coo. 'It's as salivation-worthy as salvation and as absolute as absolution.'

'I am hungry, your holiness.'

'I know, kannamma.'

The first handful of bitter gourd roulettes starts to sizzle in the oil. I introduce all the slices in slowly, turning them all over with the ladle once so they are equally coated.

'I'm only letting you stay while I cook because your baby will want to eat this in the future and you're going to have to know how to make it for her, or him.'

'The fruit of my womb craves the fruit of sin – imagine!'

'And what is the fruit of sin?'

'Don't expect me to philosophize when I'm ravenous.'

How distractingly beautiful my friend is, I think, with her heavy belly and her palpable delight. I wink at her. 'Looks like you've already taken a bite, babe.'

And then she throws back her head and cackles at her own joke – 'Paavi! Sinner!'

The bitter gourd has started to brown. I scoop dry chilli powder, earthy red and explosive, into the concoction, and stir. I add water, and steam rises dracontine from the saucepan. And then, the second most vital ingredient: fragments of jaggery, which melt quickly and coagulate into a sticky blackness.

I stir, and stir. I taste and add – spice here, then sweetness, the bitterness itself intrinsic. Precious, for all the passion it provides. Water.

I catch something like a benison humming in my throat and salt springs to my eyes. 'I love you,' I whisper – to my friend, the mother, to the food I am making for her, to the fact of this life that has allowed me the pleasure of feasting upon it. 'I love you.'

'Aww, I adore you, darling! Now, faster, give me mercy!' She has already served herself steamed rice from the cooker by the Athangudi mosaic, and holds the plate out beseechingly. The silver butterflies at her ears allure in the afternoon light. I switch the stove off and ladle a large portion of its contents on to her plate: dark and intense, fiery, viscidly demanding, sweet as the sins that were worth the fall, bitter as deceived goodness. Bitter gourd that tastes of love and all its consequences.

It is my simplest, most sincere dish: my heart on a platter.

'This is an epiphany,' she grins, her nose running, her back resting against the spice cabinet.

I watch her for a few moments before reaching to serve myself.

With her clean hand, she grabs mine. 'Thank you!'

'Anytime, my love.' I squeeze her hand, drop the spoon I reached for, and decide to wait. What a pleasure it is to give.

Sometimes a meal is a psalm. Sometimes it is a code, a consolation, a sense of an unbroken coast in a season of ravages. Always, it is an offering. Always, it is an embrace.

## CONSORT

$P$lace your foot on the threshold. You who surrendered will not be unbroken. You who were broken will not be unexonerated. These are the coastlines, these are the borderlands, these are the purlieus which you imagined were your original syntax, your native tongue. Beyond you, all is wilderness. Within you, all is wilderness.

And he will come to you then, in that beyond. He will deliver you there, in that within. Mountain-lion bearing your viscera between his teeth. The lord of the liminal, arriving at twilight, his body like yours the battlefield, the battle your consciousness itself. Do not be afraid. You have already been severed. Let him reach into the sundering and return you to yourself. Let him place you on the bloody benediction of his lap, for it is you – and only you – who is his mountain-heart.

## BOYFRIEND LIKE
## A BANYAN TREE

I want a boyfriend like a banyan tree. A man who's a forest unto himself, with conspiracies of birds, and secret blossoms, and shaded places; a matrix generous enough for the world.

And into this forest I will wander, a beloved of the world, and walk beneath the aegis of his boughs knowing that the same love that roots them raises me. I will become entangled. I'll hang a swing from his shoulders and spend all my life in his lap, swaying from pleasure to pleasure to pleasure. I'll press my face to his ancient heart and be consoled that contained within it are all my silences. And my quietest hopes, gossamer like the wings of fig wasps.

He will sustain me as he sustains the terrain of his presence. I will step into his solitude like a miracle and smudge him sacred.

I'll rub my limbs with earth and fall asleep in the adoration of his arms. I'll taste the rain from his bark and the wind from his stranglers and invent a susurrus language. I'll count myself among his roots, adventitious, and lift my scented wrists to him and say, 'Smell me.' And when he says I have a mouth like a Christ flower and cheekbones for which the continental kiss was invented, I'll ask him to prove the heart's hagiography. I'll peer through his leaves at the marmalade moon, and if he keeps very still, I'll sing.

He'll be too good to let go, too abiding to outgrow.

And like this I will thrive, a wild and tender and cherished eloquence. Pollen-drenched and petal-hipped, lulled by his breath, a perfect still-water reflection. I'll braid my hair into his and merge into his meditation, safe and gently swaying.

From pleasure to pleasure to pleasure.

## SWEETNESS, WILDNESS, GREED

In the faithless electricity of the evening before the hunt, I stood in the verandah of the house we had borrowed at the periphery of Cloud Mountain and watched the creature that had alighted on the underside of the paper lantern, its incandescent volitation. Its upper wings were an ashen dun. Its lower ones were tigrine: warm orange with symmetrical beauty marks, and a black beachcomber fringe ink-dropped with white.

When it held them closed, it was small and camouflaged, subtle. When it opened its wings, it was an epiphany.

Mazhai came up behind me and wrapped his arm around my waist and said, 'It's called a fruit-piercer.'

'It's half moth, half monarch butterfly,' I said. I turned to him and the dusk light striped him in shadow and Cointreau. I smiled when he kissed my temple. He slipped his fingers into mine and for a while we watched the caretaker's wife swing a brazier of burning neem leaves as she walked the grounds, releasing plumes of smoke to dissuade the mosquitoes. Under her breath, she was singing.

'You go into the mountain tomorrow,' he said. I nodded.

There was a small silence. 'I'll be here.'

'I know,' I said, and squeezed his hand back.

~

Cloud Mountain is on the great Western Ghats, shielded equally from the torrents of the south-western monsoons and the torrid summers of the plains. Everywhere in this region, the roads circle up the ranges, and under the canopy of leaf-sieved sunflashes and the embrace of crisp montane air, the drive is exquisite. Leaving is complicated.

I had told Mazhai I would meet him here, so that we could travel separately on days that better suited our schedules. So the night on the bus to Mettupalayam was all mine, the winding delight of the taxi up was all mine, and one day and a night at the small stone guesthouse with the welcoming verandah were all mine. The truth is, I could have waited, and come with him. But this was the way I wanted it: solitude, to speak to no one, the songs I wanted alone on the long and lovely journey.

The first time I had come to Cloud Mountain, I had been chasing a vision.

I didn't know Mazhai then. I was itinerant; I sought myself, and was as startled by betrayals as I would be at an unreflecting mirror. I was in a fugue time in which every turn carried the delicate danger of a single raindrop hovering above the perfect catenary of a spider's web.

In this fragility, I had been longing for the sight of a man climbing up a tree, or swinging down a precipice, risking his life in the pursuit of honey. For months, the image came to me in moments when I raised my eyes from books or as I fell asleep, and I felt compelled by it. I don't think I expected salvation to come from anywhere, yet I surrendered to each possibility as completely as if I did.

I had come to Cloud Mountain, and been granted this vision, and I had sustained the memory of it through the years that followed: through caves and surfacings, a meandering route that eventually led me back. This time, with Mazhai in tow – Mazhai who is my lover but whom I still fear to name myself *beloved by*. Mazhai who says he will wait for me, has always been waiting for me, who will sit and read on a verandah as I trek into the forest if that is what will make me happy. 'Whisper my name on the other side of the mountain, and I'll hear your voice, you know that,' he says into my hair as we fall asleep that night. From him, it is more than a sweet nothing. I am capricious, moon-coxswained, but his is a manifest clarity and he has placed me – he says, and says again and again – at its heart.

~

In the morning, I meet the five honeygatherers at the bus station. I have bought them packets of lunch, water, cigarettes – frankly-requested perks which I don't think twice about, for the privilege as I see it is truly only mine. This is a meeting that was planned over numerous phone calls, directly and through intermediaries from the non-governmental organization that supports them. The last of these was from the guesthouse last night, and until the moment when I see Jadayan, the oldest honeygatherer, I hadn't been aware that I had been chanting silently, or how nervous I had been that this would not happen at all.

The first time they took me on an expedition was pure kismet. I had come to Cloud Mountain after corresponding with the organization, had spent a morning among their archives, and been told apologetically that there was no real guarantee about being able to go into the forest. I saw giant honeycombs in the library and idly sifted through my disappointment. The apis dorsata, the bee that crafts its hives on cliffs, was what I might have seen, if I had been allowed to join an expedition. I thought I identified more closely with the apis cerana, with its shy queen who likes her darkness. But just as I was about to leave the office, I was literally met at the threshold by two men holding a large plastic bag of beeswax between them.

'When are you next going to hunt honey?' the officer beside me asked.

'Not today, not tomorrow, not anytime this week,' said one of the men.

'She' – I was nodded at – 'leaves the day after tomorrow.'

There was a moment of silence, of looking into faces, and then the man who would be introduced to me as Jadayan spoke – 'We'll take you tomorrow then.'

Now, seeing Jadayan fills me with elation. I press my palms together and then take a single one of his in my hands and squeeze it.

'Nobody else has come yet?'

'No, not yet.'

'They will come.' He sits down and lights a cigarette, and we wait. In the next ten minutes, Rangar, the actual collector of the honey himself, and Seyyon and Veylan arrive separately. Seyyon and Veylan, in whose grips Rangar entrusts his life at the cliff, are no longer the boys I remember, but young men. Recently married, both of them, they tell me shyly on the bus later. I am touched that they remember me, that their familiar smiles indicate that they had placed my name when I called. They enquire after my mother. I enquire after their families and the hamlet I visited in which Rangar and Seyyon reside.

Rangar's mother had sung, just for me, traditional songs of parting before a hunt, of a wife's fear and a husband's reassurance, or a husband's trepidation and a wife's encouragement.

'To seek sweetness is your fate,' went one. 'To wait for it, my lord, is mine.'

Mazhai in the stone cottage, reading the newspaper, throwing sticks for the dog to fetch, taking an hour's bus to another hill station to see a museum or a waterfall perhaps. Filling his time until I return for dinner, carrying the forest back for him.

At Queens Shola, twenty minutes away, a

shorter drive than the wait for the bus itself, we disembark. It is about eleven in the morning, and the sun is a guñelve of sheer whiteness in the clear summer sky. Here, we enter the tea estate with its staggered copper-sulphate blue houses, a small village step-cut into the hill, walking up the well-worn footpath and then directly into the plantation, vivid with tea leaves.

We are going back to Kakula Parai, the same place they brought me to years ago. Again, this summer, there is honey there – they have sighted it already, mapped its presence, for reconnaissance and gathering happen separately. Once again, the harvesting season is almost over – it is the end of May – and I find that 'serendipity' is an inadequate word.

We trek through the tea bushes and arrive at the clearing at the entrance of the forest. I do not know what fauna we will encounter, but in this calmness, I can hear the jiragavalli puchi, the insect that cries all day then dies, and the crooning of that most dulcet of birds, the kuyil.

Jadayan turns to me. 'This time you've worn your own pottu, Shyama.' He gestures delicately at the vermilion between my eyebrows and smiles. 'But wear one from the forest too, won't you?' He breaks a leaf off by the stem and dots the sap on my face too. It is a gesture of protection, but also – and I hope I'm not imagining this, casting my own journey's significance into the everyday toil of other lives – perhaps a gesture of tenderness.

~

The forest gives; we only receive.

Prayer is the first and final duty. Every expedition is a ritual, and it begins with the seeking and securing of permission. In the clearing, there is a small black rock, an irregular triangle, anointed with holy ash. It is always here, beneath a tree not far from where a small stream flows. This is the natural border between forest and not-forest. At this checkpoint, incense sticks are lit and pinned into a comb of bananas and placed before the guardian of the temenos as an offering. Jadayan sings and chants in Irula, and then a camphor flame is also offered, first to the deity and then to the rest of us. We hold our fingertips over it and bring its heat to our eyes, three times, quickly.

The prayer at the border completed, Jadayan squats by the brook and begins to dig into the earth with his bare hands. I squat by his side and join him, relishing the pleasure of the cool soil. A few resolute scoops in, clear water begins to pool

– cleaner than the stream's, though from the same source. It is cold and sweet on the tongue. 'Do you remember this?' he asks as we dig. 'Yes, of course,' I say. 'And now we will have tea.'

Veylan and Seyyon create a makeshift fire, over which tea is brewed using the water Jadayan has excavated. We have brought with us a few tools – knives, matchboxes and a pan among them – some items of nourishment, and bottles to carry the honey home.

'Shyama Akka,' says Seyyon. 'The first time you came was the first time I went on a honey hunt too. But I've come back every year since.' Off-season, he goes on, he takes on contractual labour and coolie work in Ooty. His wife sells vegetables. He will be a father for the first time in October.

'I haven't come back every year since,' I try to make a joke. Sometimes, my guilt and ignorance made me awkward. There are crevices in the ways in which we experience the world that cannot always be bridged simply.

'I told you you'd come back to the mountain,' says Jadayan, very seriously.

'You did,' I say. I hesitate to tell him that the other thing he had told me, that I would not fall ill for five years after my visit to Cloud Mountain's healing clime and medicinal herbs, did not come true – I had nearly died later that year, the year I first visited. But I take a jagged breath and decide to let it go. What matters is that I am still here.

A second round of tea is poured for those who want it. We open the newspaper-wrapped packets of lunch: each contains rice and potato curry, some fried okra, a large crushed pappadum. The food is no longer warm, but tastes good, and I am glad – when I had bought it from behind the bus depot, I hadn't even known what the pre-packed parcels would contain.

'Is your husband not as fearless as you are?' asks Veylan. 'Why didn't he come to the forest too?'

I shouldn't be surprised that word had spread that I had travelled with a man, but I suppose it's the word itself I am hung up on. I shouldn't correct him; I remind myself that in many people's eyes, by writ of virtue and custom, Mazhai is indeed my husband. 'No no, he is brave,' I waver. He is, it's true. 'He just wanted to take a holiday, he doesn't like to trek. He likes to read and write.'

'The mountain didn't call him,' says Jadayan. 'Amaippu ille.'

But how do you know, I wonder silently. Maybe the mountain had called him, but it was I – my qualms, my hesitations – who had thwarted him. Should he be here too?

'It's just something I need to do myself, you know?' I'd explained to him, once when I first decided I would go back to Cloud Mountain, once as I prepared to take the overnight bus, and once yesterday.

'I know,' he'd said, each time, and asked no further questions.

But here, finally in the forest, I am not certain of either thing: what it was I had needed to do, and why it was I had wanted to do it without him. I'm not alone, I think, looking around me as my guides wash their hands and wipe their mouths. It was never about being alone.

~

In the early days of our courtship, I told Mazhai the story of how I had gone to Cloud Mountain for no reason other than that I felt I had to see it for myself: honey.

'What drove you, woman?' he asked. We were in bed, languid and happy, sharing hours and hours of indolence. That was something delicious, something I couldn't recall savouring ever. Passion fades; but the trust that comes from lavishly idled time is precious. 'That's…' and he turned me to him by the waist and crinkled his brow, 'pretty intense.'

'Sweetness.' I kissed one closed eye. 'Wildness.' I kissed the other. 'And,' – and here I bit his nose – 'greed.'

He smiled. 'That's a long way to travel for a single word, or even for three.'

'I've travelled a lot further for a lot less.'

'Oh really? Where'd you go?'

But the words were muffled, re-sheathed in a blur of pressed noses and sticky kisses. I would tell him later, and he would tell me. The scars we limned on each other were never used as amatory stratagem.

How completely can you know a person? For years, my closest friends were my most important relationships – our significant others, we called one another frankly. When I met Mazhai, nothing changed. He became one more significant other, but the one with whom one further dimension existed. It was not physicality per se – I think of the friend whose feet I draw on with a ballpoint pen as we talk on a couch or a bed, the friend who always kisses my shoulder as we hug goodbye, the friend who holds my hand as we walk on the beach: love is not only its demonstrations, but is always in them. Desire, of course – with Mazhai there is desire (and satisfaction!). But there is something that's even one interior step deeper. If

I could name it I would. It is as though in me, all my life, were cenotes, reservoirs of beauty and splendour I had kept and tended and known not for whom. He came into this life as though he had always been a part of it.

Through a long decade of loneliness, I learnt to try to see every exchange as an act of human circuitry, a glimmer in the live wire that connects us all. Jadayan and his men are preparing to fashion the devices of the hunt from scratch. In almost all ways, I am useless: I am inexperienced, physically weaker, and not a man. I am not from their tribe, I have merely bought a day of their ordinary lives like an ore I can set into the breccia of my own. And the work of honeygathering is a thousand years old, and it has no need for spurious traditions like good luck charms, decoys or ceremonial guardians – all things a girl can be, perhaps. But not this girl, not here or ever.

So I am their guest – the guest of the mountain, Jadayan would correct me if I spoke this thought aloud. And I sit quietly on the forest floor and watch as they begin assembling the tools. There are four specific types of equipment and each must be made from scratch for every expedition: a ladder, a contrivance known as a kukketappa in which the hive is collected, a wooden spear with which to dislodge the hives from the surface of the cliff and a panthai, a bundle of leaves which will be set fire to so as to smoke out the bees. The forest provides what is necessary.

And most necessary of all is rope. Most of it is created from the fibre of the biskoti vine, flexible and abundant in the forest, or from the climbers of the flowering karasamaram. The bark is removed with a knife, which peels away in lengthy spirals. Rangar takes it in his hands and twists it himself, weaving the ladder from which he will swing against the sheer face of the cliff.

Seyyon and Veylan, the young ones, are responsible for gathering the materials. After they have brought the biskoti and karasamalai, they go back to collect tree branches, and then long and long-stemmed leaves from the upper reaches of trees, including the kolimaram, with its flowers that smell a little like forest jasmine, or perhaps moringa. When Rangar's ladder has been finished, Seyyon takes shorter lengths of the biskoti and readies them for knot-making: to tie tree branches into a Y-shaped formation for the kukketappa, and to secure the leaves into a panthai.

At the base of a nearby tree, covered in a pile of leaves, is an open tin box. It had been left there after the last harvest. This is a custom: some honey is always given to the forest first, in the same way the sacred rivers are given offerings of water. Jadayan retrieves this box. It is tied to the aperture of the Y-shaped prong of branches the boys have assembled, the only non-organic material in the entire hunt, the only implement that is not made afresh. This becomes the kukketappa. It will catch the honey, and then become the vessel in which it is given back to the forest.

A lengthy branch, fortified with a more slender one, becomes the spear with which the hives will be prodded from the cliff. Depending on the angle and size, they will drop into the kukketappa or thud to the ground below, near where Jadayan will be sitting cross-legged.

For the panthai, the smoker, a dry grass they call Bombaypul is parcelled out and wrapped in fresh green leaves. Held aloft, the bundles are twined together with long grass and spun in the air so that the knotting becomes secure. Then, the panthai is tied to another long measure of twined biskoti.

'Where will you wait this time?' asks Rangar. 'Down below or beside Jadayan Saami?'

The first time, there had been a sixth member in our expedition, another boy who had been dispatched mainly to look after me. He and I had waited and watched the harvesting at a slight distance, from the entrance of a bear's night cave. Jadayan was at the base of the cliff, a hundred metres ahead of us. And dangling over its sheer face like a pendant was Rangar, nothing between him and certain death but his grip on the rope ladder and the grace of the mountain.

'I'll decide once we're there.'

'Are you hoping to meet a bear this time?'

'Maybe a leopard!' I laugh.

'You are braver than before.'

I simply smile in response.

The apparatus are all ready, and we venture deeper into the forest, hacking our way past scraggly shrubbery. My tunic catches bramble and tears a little, but I was prepared for this. Along the way I am instructed to collect leaves and dry grasses, which Seyyon cuts or pulls off for me. I carry them in a too-small bundle of cloth in my arms, trying to keep them from scratching my face.

~

Kakula Parai, the cliff where our journey culminates, rises into view. Three dark hives cling to the underside of a shallow overhang at its top.

For one vivid moment, I lose my sense of balance. All of it comes back to me: the questions, the terror, the way all birth – even rebirth – is trauma. And with it, the renewed notion of all of life itself as a pilgrimage. I have come here once before. I have lived long enough to come back. The extent of this miracle is mine alone to truly know, but who I share it with – this wildly miraculous, inordinately beautiful life – is what makes that secret, too, a gift.

'Beliajhen!' I shout, and my companions applaud. *Big honey!* It is the Irula word for the rich, heavy hives; I am simply imitating what Jadayan taught me the first time, pointing his cigarette skyward.

He grins, and I'm not sure whether he asks a question or makes a command, but when he says, 'You will sit with me,' I accede with joy.

We climb up the craggy path, pass the bear cave by which I once took cover – here I kneel discreetly and touch the rocky floor and then my forehead. I am grateful. Jadayan and I stop directly within the maw formed by the outcropping at the top of the cliff. He blesses Rangar, Veylan and Seyyon very quickly. The three of them keep moving, trailing the path to the other side. Jadayan assumes his position in one corner, the hives diagonally above

him, and crosses his legs and sits. I follow him.
I look up, and the actual height of the cliff is
even more impressive from within it. It will be a
different view this time, not the panorama I saw
from the bear cave years ago. This time, I belong
in the canvas. I am not only watching. I have come,
this time, not only to take.

I open my arms and let the leaves and grasses
tumble out and take my matchbox out of my
pocket. 'I'll tell you when, wait,' says Jadayan.

Rangar, Seyyon and Veylan must complete their
ascents up the sides of the cliff. Here, they will
throw the ladder over it and Rangar will descend,
instruments in hand. In the long centuries of Irula
honeygatherers before them, Rangar's brothers-
in-law would have been made responsible for the
task of holding his ladder, because they would
never allow the singing woman waiting for him
to become a widow. From the bottom of the cliff,
on the rocky ground on which a fallen hive – or a
fallen man – will land, I consider how I have never
looked over it. What a sight it must be to stand
atop Kakula Parai.

So much is elided in a moment, let alone over
a millennium. Now, only men perform the work
of harvesting honey, but five generations ago
there was a woman – her name was Peechi – who

accepted the challenge of harvesting hives on a particularly steep cliff. Jealous of her feat, the men who had challenged her cut the rope from the tree at its peak as she climbed back. When she fell to her death, it was not without cursing the cliff range – the wax in its hives all melted, streaking the rock as though with the salt of a thousand tears. The bees of that range make honey freely; her spirit protects them, and no man dares stray near.

Mazhai is nothing like any man I'd known before him. It's a testament to how completely I withdrew from each of them that I don't fear them sleeping in a curl of his hair or in a vulpine flash of his laughing teeth or even in certain tricks of light or shadow. By the time I met him, I had left even their ghosts behind.

But the last time I was here was ominous, the cusp beyond which my life truly fell from my grasp for a long spell. Forgetting is neither simple nor without consequence. I remember the quiet devastation I felt as I left Cloud Mountain then: so completely unsalvaged that even the unseasonal downpour that accompanied my vehicle on the descent seemed to hang off the verdure like an incubus. I remember fighting so hard to give myself snatches of sweetness. So much worse was still to come, and in some ways I think I knew it already. A terrible, fierce love for that self of mine overcomes me – younger, brave, in smithereens. *Oh, Shyama, what a long way you've come.* I blink away tears. Above me, the rope ladder cascades over the brink of the cliff, and as a ripple of goosebumps rises on my skin, I count in a flash the years that followed and their teachings, the answers delivered almost acroamatically, and I decide to release all of it – loss and learning, claim and abandonment – into the elements. What did I come to the forest for if not this?

They were not mountains, those men. Only arêtes, and they knifed into me and left vast, dark valleys.

But *only one mountain can know the core of another mountain.* Frida Kahlo wrote that. And she knew.

'Get ready to light the fire,' says Jadayan.

And then he begins to sing – loudly, shoutingly – to the bees so that they will return the following year and remake their great gold-hearted hives, to the cliff that harbours them, to the forest that allows and excludes as it chooses, and to the god of the forest who is also the forest who is God.

Slowly, Rangar emerges over Kakula Parai, rung by rung, the wooden spear in one hand, the kukketappa in the other. He is completely unarmoured. When he has reached a comfortable position, the panthai – already burning – is lowered. It swings dangerously close to the hives, smoke trailing from it like a seduction.

'Now,' Jadayan says to me, and I don't know what happens first – that I strike two matches in quick succession and light the pile of leaves between us, or that a great dark torrent – accompanied by a loud and engulfing drone – has taken over the landscape.

In a matter of seconds, they are all around us: intoxicated bees, drunk on smoke, driven from their hives, debilitated of the senses but still capable – should they want to – of stinging. A cloud of thousands of honeybees, in stupor but in flight.

And through this confusion of smoke and bees we can see him, Rangar, precariously dangling on a ladder of vines, prodding at each hive with his spear. Graceful as a trapeze artist, he manoeuvres in mid-air, his feet and legs gripping the ladder as his arms stretch out to tease the hive away from the rock.

Jadayan continues to sing. I am wordless by his side, made silent with emotion.

Rangar prods at the largest hive slowly, swinging close. He works its stickiness away from the rock surface with his spear – does it truly come away so easily, or is his exertion overshadowed by the sheer choreography of his movements: arms full of instruments, feet entangled in twine, the reel and sway of the ladder, his lifeline?

The hive drops to the floor, not far from where we sit, with a loud thud. Jadayan gestures for me to leave it be and to keep fanning the fire.

There are two more to go, and each must be given the same attention. For a moment I see Rangar hesitate, and I know somehow that he is wondering whether to pass the kukketappa back to Seyyon and Veylan and let the remaining hives also fall. It will give him a free hand. But he chooses against it, and cautiously nudges the second hive with the spear. This time, he manages to collect it cleanly in the tin box of the kukketappa.

The panthai swings in a loop again and the bees agitate anew at this trespass.

I fan the flames of the burning leaves, inciting larger plumes.

Rangar performs the same elegant set of actions, cleaving the last hive from the rock. Each time, he raises the kukketappa to safety: one boy reaching over a little further to take the hive and store it on the plateau while Rangar continues to swing, a halo of honeybees around him.

And then, when the overhang has been stripped

of its richness for this year, Jadayan sings more words of praise, and Rangar climbs back to the top of Kakula Parai.

And then we make our way back down into the forest clearing, carrying those beautiful black hives. There is not a sting on any one of us, not this time.

~

Once again, I sit on the forest floor, its bed rustling wherever I touch it, and watch as the harvest begins, the hunt successful.

The hives are shorn of excess – larvae and young brood, but not wax, are among what is edible – and cut into manageable pieces. These pieces are wrapped in fine cloth and squeezed by hand. Fresh honey, darkly golden, pours out from these sieves and into the tins and bottles that have been carried here from the villages, from civilization.

One piece is placed inside the tin box, now dismantled from the kukketappa, and dedicated to the forest. It is kept at the foot of the same tree it was taken from.

When the cloths are opened, clusters of tipsy bees still cling to the drained portions. I touch one very delicately and it barely quivers. How vulnerable it is, how ferocious. These are flung back into the shrubbery; the bees will sober up and carry on.

I am in a sort of devotion-drunk euphoria. I am not sure who it is who cuts away a small piece of fresh honeycomb, wraps it in a leaf, and gives it to me.

It is just like I remembered it: bitter mountain honey, dark honey that comes from the nectar of the black plum flower.

And I smile as much for its taste as for the memory of my first, extraordinary bite of raw honeycomb. Back then, that long-ago evening, I had called it a complicated, intense taste to suit a complicated, intense experience. And as the men continued to wring the combs, I had sat there in silence on the dry leaves of the forest floor and enjoyed a few moments of true, raw wonderment.

But how simple it all really is.

Bitter and sweet honey, bitter and sweet like my very heart.

~

Natural light has almost run out by the time we reach the tea estate; but tonight the moon too is a completed circle, and as we weave through the lower reaches of the bushes we can see its early ascent: enormous behind the quickly silhouetting trees, its colour almost pure aurum. We must hurry through the streets lined with the blue houses of the estate's workers, make our way to the bus stand in time for the 7.45 p.m. bus so we will not need to stand there another hour, shivering.

We make it, we are early by ten minutes or so, carrying all our bags and bottles evenly between us. The bus stand is only a road marker, and these are final moments: for promises, for thanks, for all that can be said even when no words are adequate.

'Will you come see us in Anil Kaadu?' I think of the beautiful hamlet of six thatched roofs in which Rangar lives, named for the flying giant Malabar squirrels that can still be seen leaping between the high branches of the area's trees. It has its own private vista, a stunning range of cliffs in the near distance. At the entrance of the hamlet is a shrine to Kattraya, who carries honey, who by any other name is the heart of the forest herself.

The forest is changing; its animals grow smaller in number, even the people who belong to it venture further and further away, even if only in ever-flaring loops.

I belong to the forest. It is here I came to console myself. It is here I have come in thanksgiving.

I say yes to the question – I imagine Mazhai and me visiting tomorrow with gifts of provisions and confectionery, being able to listen to Rangar's mother, Malakshmi, sing. What will she sing for us; what will she sing for me when I already know, deep down, all the songs of parting?

It is too dark by the time we board the bus to see much of the route. It's mostly empty and because we are all tired, we take individual rows. Jadayan smiles deeply at me once from the far front of the bus, then turns away and rests his head against the window railings. Behind me, Rangar falls into a quick slumber. Seyyon and Veylan make small talk for a few minutes but even that gives way to cicada undersong and the sounds of the heavy vehicle on the ragged roads. Night buses are slower, necessarily, but quieter too. The night falls differently in the forests and the mountains; a sweet-scented and wild goddess roams, I am certain of it, and at the threshold of twilight she reclaims her dwelling, demands respect.

'You're very blessed,' the officer at the Adivasi interests' organization, with its great dark honeycombs behind preserved glass, had told me years ago, after that fortuitous meeting at the doorstep with Jadayan and Rangar. It is a word I fought so long to feel. A word like loved, or beloved, or beauty – an immense, empirical intangible.

'So far to travel for a single word, or even three,' my beloved had said to me once, not so long ago. I think of him waiting for me, not even an hour away, a dog or two at his feet, mosquitoes nibbling at his lovely limbs, an aura of monarch moths around the home that for a few nights is ours. And I am warmer than the wool I have around my shoulders on this lightly piercing Nilgiri night. I watch through the railings of the bus until we take a turn and the mountain disappears behind us, and then, as each of the men I have travelled with disembarks, I find myself alone on the route's last stretch. I take a profoundly grateful breath and imagine it: the full moon over the tea estate, a leopard threading a sovereign path through the bushes, placing its paws almost reverently, gently on the good earth.

## ACKNOWLEDGEMENTS

I am grateful to the editors of the following journals and anthologies, in which the following stories have appeared.

*The Affair* – 'Sweet'; *Baker's Dozen* (Tranquebar Press, 2013) – 'Greed and the Gandhi Quartet'; *Bengal Lights* – 'The Black Widow'; *Best of the Net 2013* (Sundress Publications, 2013) – 'Nine Postcards from the Pondicherry Border'; *ELLE India* – 'Greed and the Gandhi Quartet'; *Erotique* – 'Sky Clad'; *The Female Complaint* (Shade Mountain Press, 2015) – 'The High Priestess Never Marries'; *Flycatcher* – 'Nine Postcards from the Pondicherry Border'; *Hobart* – 'Afternoon Sex'; *Jaggery* – 'Corvus'; *Monkeybicycle* – 'Take the Weather with You'; *The Moth* – 'Sweet'; *Not Somewhere Else But Here* (Sundress Publications, 2014) – 'Nine Postcards from the Pondicherry Border'; *Out Of Print* – 'The High Priestess Never

Marries'; *Pure Slush* – 'Gigolo Maami'; *Spry* – 'Salomé'; *Rose Red Review* – 'Sandalwood Moon'; *Verity La* – 'Self-portrait without Mythology'; *Wyvern Lit* – 'Menagerie'; *Whiskeypaper* – 'Boyfriend Like a Banyan Tree'.

To everyone at HarperCollins India who made this book possible.

Special thanks to Jadayan, Chinnasami, J. Murugan, C. Murugan and R. Krishnan, and to Keystone Foundation (Kotagiri).

And most of all, to my friends, who know who they are.